෨ *The River Front* ෫

Fiction Series
The Alex Evercrest Series
The River Front
The Girl on The Grill
Missing
Maggot
Racist
Votive Candles
Windy City
Country Road
Pool of Blood
Sins of the Daughter
Body Parts
The Skull Collector
The Vanishing
The Shadow Fighter
Moonshine
Grief's Trajectory
The Magic Touch
Northern Lights
Alex Evercrest Heroine
Alex Evercrest Collection Two
New Direction
A Family Affair
Disruption
The St. Lebuinnus Church Murder

A Brian O'Neil Novel
Hawaiian Phoenix
Moon Curser
Death Broker

The Problem Solver Series
Solutions
Drug Lords
Border Crosser
The Problem Solver Collection

The Taelo Series
Taelo: The Early Years
Taelo: The Golden Feather
Taelo: Journey of Discovery
Taelo: Dangerous Passage
Taelo: Condor Clan Slingers
Taelo: Circumvention
Taelo: The Journey of Sages
Taelo: Collection
Taelo: Future Leaders Journey

A Taelo Story:
White Swan and Quiet Pheasant
The Child's Name
Floating Cloud
Quiet Rabbit
Busy Bee
Little Otter & Talking Wren
Broken Spear
Burley Bear & Meadow Flower
Taelo Story Collection

Science Fiction

The Savitar Series:
Journey's End
Savitar
Confluence
Savitar Series Collection

Bram Nielson Series
The Fold
The Message
Fold Wormhole
Negative Fold
Ripples in Time
Bram Nielson Collection

<u>Single Science Fiction Books:</u>
Current Past and Future
The Event
The Door
Viajante 7

Ron Mueller

❧ *The River Front* ☙
By: *Ron Mueller*

Around the World Publishing LLC
Cincinnati, Ohio

Ron Mueller

The River Front ©

ISBN 13: 978-1-68223-327-6

Distributed by Ingram
Alex Evercrest Model By: Pi03@ShutterStock
Cincinnati Scene: Nagel Photography @ShutterStock
Cover Design By: Ron Mueller

Dedicated to the wonderful family that has enriched my life.

Ron Mueller

Table of Contents

Ron Mueller

1 The Invalid Marathon Runner

Dianne ran uphill toward a tall scrawny old man that carried a long walking stick and was descending along the trail. The winding trail was little more than a path that was originally formed over the years by the deer.

It was clear to her that he was not going to step off the trail to let her by. She was tempted to run into him and knock him over. She thought better since he was at least twice her size, armed with his walking stick, and coming down hill.

At the last moment he stepped to one side. She was so surprised that she forgot to thank him. She heard him shout "thank you" behind her. Yeah, you too, she though with a snarl running through her mind. Then she let out a verbal growling snarl. She so hated to be corrected by ignorant adults.

Where the trail reached the peak and turned along a ridge to the right, she normally turned and went back the way she had come up. She did not want to catch up to the old man, so she went to the right along the ridge. This was a rougher and more difficult return route. There was a small stream that was impossible to cross without getting her shoes wet.

She was wearing her new shoes that she had scrounged and saved for. Saving for them had taken her almost two years.

She was not about to get them wet.

When she got to the stream she stopped and took off her shoes and socks and waded across the cool clear stream.

The water felt great.

She sat down with her feet in the water and thought about her parents.

Neither of her parents were aware that she had bought the shoes. They knew she ran every day and had questioned whether she was getting her homework done.

She did both.

Her parents were aware of her running ability and quietly encourage her to keep doing it. They were barely getting by and seeing her daughter seemingly happy and prospering in school and its activities helped ease their financial frustrations.

Her running had caught the eye of the track coach. She had put Dianne on her long-distance running team.

Her art had caught her art teacher's eye. He had encouraged her and had sponsored her in several art shows.

Dianne embraced the help coming from school more than the questions and what she interpreted as a lack of support from her parents.

Dianne though of her mother as a borderline alcoholic. Her mother's drinking was the cause of many arguments that went on with her father.

Her father was a UPS delivery driver. She thought that the work kept him in decent shape and that he made enough so that they should have been moving up the economic ladder. She blamed her mother's drinking and spending habits that ensured that the family would be renting the same house that they had been renting since the two had been married.

Dianne was ecstatic when she received a scholarship offer from a small college in the northeast. It was known for its track team and for turning out artists and art curators.

She eagerly moved from the Ohio to the Northeast.

Her time at the University was a blur but she became her own woman. She made few friends but did well in her classes and excelled in the long-distance running.

The running kept her in shape, and since the scholarship was based on her athletic ability it made it possible for her to stay at the university.

Her painting skills were good, her other skills such as pottery, carving, and metal working were adequate, but they were of little interest to her.

It soon became clear that she loved to curate and organizing the numerous tasks associated with the role. She excelled in organizing exhibits and writing the labels that explained and interpreted the art. She knew that she had found her career knitch. It was a realization that eased her mind.

She noted that she was not a fast enough long-distance runner when in several marathons, she ended up in the middle of the pack.

She learned she was an endurance runner when she placed third in a thirty-five-mile ultra-marathon. She was now looking toward trying out a hundred-mile ultra-marathon. She knew she had a chance to be number one or two at the worst. She could run all day. She knew that if she finished first a few times she would be able to land some advertising spots that would lead to an income that would eliminate the need to get an eight to four curator's job.

Graduation came too quickly. She landed a position in a small art museum in Kentucky and accepted it when it became apparent that she had only received the one offer.

She laughed at her lifestyle changes. She had grown up in Ohio. She had found herself in the Northeast and was now going to make her living in Kentucky.

At least the area around the small town had large hills that were almost small mountains and provided her a good training area to prepare her for long-distance running.

She ran the Cincinnati Flying Pig marathon and did well enough in it and two other marathons that she got accepted to the Boston Marathon.

Preparing for the Boston Marathon became her singular focus. Work did not suffer but it always seemed to last too long. She craved the wind blowing through her hair as she ran.

Her Boston Marathon was memorable. She had not expected to be in the top running group but did come in the top twenty percent group.

She celebrated by having a lobster dinner at a harbor side restaurant.

The visits to at least a half dozen museums made the trip memorable. It motivated her to seek a more challenging curator position.

On her return from the Boston Marathon, she took several classes at the University of Kentucky and sent out numerous job applications.

She felt lucky to be interviewed and then landing the curator's position at the Taft Museum of Art in Cincinnati.

Things seemed to be going up for her.

As part of her acceptance of the Taft Museum job offer, she negotiated time off to run in the Chicago Marathon. She had been planning on it even before running the Boston Marathon. She had been in training for the entire time since then.

She rented an apartment within walking distance of the Taft Museum. The work was pleasant, and the work atmosphere was positive, but she worked so she could run.

Her move to Cincinnati had eaten up her savings so she contemplated postponing her Chicago Marathon participation.

She ran the Circleville Ultra-Marathon as a warm-up for the Chicago Marathon.

She was elated to come in second. She was disappointed that there were no advertising offers.

She then focused on the Chicago Marathon and ran all the hills that Cincinnati and the surrounding area provided.

She felt super about her chances at placing high in the marathon. She had been running faster and she was in the best shape of her life.

She took time off and drove to Chicago and stayed far enough from the race area to get a hotel at a reasonable price. This event was going to zero out her savings and most probably max out her credit card, but she was sure it would be worth it.

On the morning of the race, she took a taxi to the starting point. She was feeling great and hoping to place in the top ten percent of the participants. She knew that the Chicago Marathon was one of the biggest races and attracted many of the top runners from around the world. Her goal was to do well enough so she could land a few sponsors that would provide the money to equip and pay for her formal training.

She was so motivated that it gave her an adrenaline high.

She was far enough back in the pack that when the sound of the gun signaled the start of the race, she had to wait for those in the front to start moving before she had a chance to take a step.

This slow start raised her level of anxiety.

Once the field spread and the running began, she continually passed runners and worked herself toward the front of the group.

The runners began to thin out and maneuvering room allowed her to continually move toward the front. Soon she was sure she was closing in on the top ten percent. This group was in a long thin line.

Her movement forward continued until she approached a group all wearing the same team outfits that were spread out in a flat line that kept other runners like herself from moving beyond them.

She worked back and forth behind them trying to break through.

She was frustrated and super mad.

This was a team tactic to allow one of their team members somewhere ahead toward the front to do well.

By marathon rules, it was also supposed to be illegal.

She saw an opening and made a move to get through. Suddenly she felt someone step on her heel. Her forward step was missing the leg that had been stepped on. She saw the street curb coming up at her. She heard the cracking of bones as she hit the curb hip first and then her head hit, and the world went black.

When she opened her eyes, she felt the air being delivered to her nose. She realized that she was in a hospital bed.

She was immediately angry. That runner had stepped on her foot. He not only should be disqualified but punished. She intended to sue.

She called the marathon organizer to file a complaint on the runner that tripped her. She told them that she wanted his name and that she planned to sue him or her.

The organizer replied that the accident had been recorded. It clearly showed that she had stepped in front of the runner in question and that the blame for the accident was hers.

After a brief shouting match, she hung up.

She was beyond being angry. She was furious and she vowed that somehow; she would get even.

Her vow portended something well beyond getting even and subsequent events would slowly turn that vow into something more sinister than getting even.

She remained in the hospital for more than a month.

She hired a driver to drive her home in her car. Paying for a month of parking once again made her angry.

She was in a wheelchair and unable to stand and walk. The surgeon that had repaired her hip informed her that she would most likely never run again.

This made her angrier. It was like being told that she had lost her best friend.

He connected her with a Cincinnati doctor to guide her rehabilitation.

Dianne was determined to return to running. She worked hard to make a comeback.

She slowly lost perspective and her connection with reality.

The pain subsided to the point that it allowed her to work but her mind became focused on her need to get even with the runner that had shattered her hip and her dreams.

She began to build the scenarios that would provide her with revenge against the long, distance male runners. In her mind that was made up by an army of guilty people. In her mind they were men that did not care about other people.

Her success in school was her ability to compartmentalize and organize each part of her life and work. This compartmenting capability helped her split her focus between work and getting revenge.

She set herself on the path to learn all she could about areas in Cincinnati where long distance runners practiced.

The river front path was only a few blocks from the Museum. She decided that she needed to get a first-hand look at the layout of the that path.

Still in her wheelchair, she wheeled the entire ten-mile length of the path.

She had a clear goal in mind and scouted out the spot where she planned to carry out her first act of revenge.

She also had no intention of getting caught. She made sure that she would be able to get to the spot she picked and then afterward retreat and leave without a trace of being there.

She did physical practice run throughs of what she planned to do. After several weeks she felt confident that she could pull off her first act of revenge.

She then selected the sites around Cincinnati and the nearby communities. Hyde Park, The Little Miami Trail, The Union Cemetery, and The Loveland Bike trail were on her list. She visited each multiple times.

At each location she selected the specific spot where her revenge would be carried out.

Her physical condition slowly improved.

She had no clue that her mental state was slowly deteriorating. Her reality changed without her knowing.

Her pain slowly decreased to the point that she was able to take a few steps.

The diagnosis from her doctor that she was making great progress bothered her. She could barely walk. If walking a few steps was great progress, then to her running became such a distant goal that it took her farther into her mental abyss.

She retreated farther into her world of getting even. A psychiatrist would have diagnosed her as a psychopath.

Now her twisted mind led her to believe that it was ok because she was just getting even by killing male runners.

She had identified the locations where she would take action.

Now she concentrated on the ways she would take the action. She needed a way that would make it impossible for her to get caught.

She thought about what she was good at and how her current capabilities could be leveraged. When her imagination produced the vision of how she could carry out her revenge she let out a laugh.

She went to the grocery store and bought two musk melons.

She drew a face and ears on each melon. She had selected an art pencil as her weapon of choice. Properly used, it would be inconspicuous, silent, and immediately effective.

Every morning, she practiced rapidly pushing her pencil into the spot on the melon ear that represented the ear canal. She would then eat the practice melon. A month later, after going through so many melons that she had lost count; she felt that her technique had been perfected.

She figured that the timing was right since she was sick of eating the melons.

The sound of her voice as she cackled with glee at the thought made her stop and look at herself in the mirror. She had expected to see herself as a witch!

Location and method in hand, she now needed to select and learn the timing of the target runners.

Each evening, she sat on the new river front family swings. She always took an end swing and parked her wheelchair to her right.

She spent the next month alternating sitting on the River Front family swings and sitting at Hyde Park's Crystal Lake in her wheelchair. She identified the runners who ran later in the evening. This was a time when each park emptied and often had no other persons but the lone runner.

She soon narrowed her target to two runners in each location.

For the next month she verified the habits of the runners she had zeroed in on. She meticulously logged their time and the variation of their time.

She also kept a keen eye for other people that wandered through the park.

She was ready and only needed to pick the date.

Luck seemed to set the opportune time for the first kill. An art appreciation fund raiser was scheduled for the coming weekend. This seemed to be a perfect cover and alibi.

She fashioned the agenda to provide a forty-five-minute window for her to execute her scheme.

She set up a drawing contest in which she too would participate. She sketched most of her entry and put it aside. She would step out when no one was paying attention and be back for the judging of the entries.

On the evening of the event, she talked to all the potential donors and introduced the contest. The top ten winners would be recognized in the Cincinnati Enquirer.

She made sure the event photographer got several shots of her talking to various dignitaries.

Finally, the moment for her to play out the river front scenario arrived.

She did not rush but quickly made her way to the river front location. She had made sure there were no security cameras on the route she took.

Her worry vanished when she observed her target run by on the way to Paul Brown stadium. His timing was perfect.

She set up her easel and placed her almost complete sketch on it. She looked around the green to ensure there was no one in sight. She walked over to the wall and as she leaned on it to relax, she dropped one of her pencils.

She looked over the wall but could not see it.

She had a moment of panic. She looked over the wall again but could not see the pencil she had dropped.

She had brought several and as she spotted her target returning, she stepped in front of the easel holding her spare pencil in hand.

She waited until it would be impossible for the runner to stop before stepping back from the easel as if to admire her work.

She was surprised at the force of the impact and would have been sent flying, but the runner caught her and together they staggered and recovered from the impact.

She laughed and asked him if he would be kind enough to render his opinion of her drawing.

The runner stepped away from her toward the easel to look.

He smiled and was just turning to say something when she rammed the pencil into his ear.

He dropped immediately. He was dead before he hit the ground.

A surge of energy went running up her back and made the hair on the back of her neck stand up.

She quickly posed him in the most embarrassing fashion that she could think of.

She looked around. Seeing no one she quickly sketched the runner onto her easel.

Then she quickly packed her sketch and easel and made her way back to the museum.

She made it back with ten minutes to spare.

She set up her easel and contest sketch and asked everyone to place theirs around the room.

Her boss and several of the crew judged the sketches. Her entry was not part of the contest, but she got several compliments on the sketch and one patron bought it as part of his donation to the gallery.

She knew that she would never be connected to the scene she had left at the river front. She smiled a enjoyed a silent cackle.

2 First Case

Her body's reflex to the ear splitting, ahooga, ahooga, blasting in her left ear launched Alex out of her bed into the dark abyss of her bedroom.

She pawed in the darkness for the phone that continued to assault her senses. She had specifically selected this sound for the calls coming from the police dispatcher. She wanted to ensure that she would immediately come awake. She gave a brief, "what's up" and listened as the dispatcher clarified that Alex and her partner were at the top of the call list. The dispatcher simply said, "there is a dead person in the River Front Park, near the Roebling bridge."

Alex came awake immediately.

This would be her first experience with leading a meaningful investigation. She and her partner had both recently joined the Cincinnati police department.

She wondered how many people had died in the park.

Was it the first?

She checked to make sure her partner had been notified and then hung up and turned on the lights.

Still barely dressed she walked to the kitchen and punched the coffee pot's brew button. Having coffee ready to brew was a practice she had started at Northwestern when she studied late into the night.

She and her partner had never worked an actual case together. She had learned from Trey that he had accepted the job offer as a way to escape what he expressed as the crazy people in Minneapolis.

He was more experienced in police work then she was but had opted to accept to be her second on their two-person team.

He was the more experienced cop, but she immediately recognized that he was on the edge of a breakdown, and he was probably drinking too much.

She learned that he had suffered PTSD from his experience in Iraq.

She knew that she would need to develop their working relationship and it would begin in earnest on this case. It was her hope to create the kind of teamwork that would take them to the head of the detective force.

She had scored one of the highest passing grades in her shooting qualification and her marshal art skills had been noted on her record.

She was petite but had trained herself to the point that she feared no one.

She also made the point of taking command of the situation when called upon.

She dressed in her bicycling clothes and rolled her bicycle out of her apartment door. She and her bike made the trip to the station every morning. It was a short five-minute ride to the station. She laughed about the fact that her "parking space" was closer to the revolving door than the Chief's.

She went into the lady's locker room and quickly changed into her field clothes comprised of a black pants suit and black leather shoes. The shoes were no nonsense black leather walking shoes.

She was now wide awake and ready for business.

She went to the dispatch area and checked about the information coming from the park. She learned that the crime unit had taped off the area, was examining the body, and taking pictures.

The reply to her question, to the dispatcher, about the number of killings in the park was that in his fifteen years on the force he had not heard of any.

Alex was sipping on her second hot cup of what was supposed to be coffee but tasted more like a sharp bitter brew of acid, when a disheveled Trey enter the detective bullpen. She groaned as she remembered that she had looked that way until she had taken responsibility and command of her life. He had the look as if he were recovering from too much drinking.

A flag went up in her mind. She chose not to say anything and concentrated on getting him up to speed and ready to get to the park.

After a quick briefing, she led the way out to their car. It was a well-kept black Ford, but it was the oldest car assigned to the detective squad. The cars were assigned based on seniority and organizational rank. She and Trey were at the bottom of the pyramid. The age of the car meant little to her. She had an old car at home that she loved.

The Chief had commented that she was lucky to have been assigned a car at all. She had laughed and replied that she would be fine riding her bike if that was what he required.

His reply was simply, "I want more out of you than riding your bike can deliver."

She looked over at Trey slouching in the passenger seat and asked if he was "Ok." His simple nod and his downward gaze told her that he was not "OK."

She drove to the park and led the way to the crime scene.

She had been told by Bill, one of the senior agents, that a crime scene work box would be required and useful. He had complemented her on being willing to listen to him when she asked to get a list of what should be in the box.

She went shopping for the items but decided that she wanted as light of a box as possible. When she was packing and organizing her box, Trevor, Bill's partner, pulled out a shiny stainless steel, crime scene work box and commented that his team had not scrimped on their box.

He pointed to and made a comment about the cheap blue plastic box she was packing.

Alex walked over to Trevor's box, picked it up and dropped it with a loud clank. She commented that Trevor's team had done so little field work that they never had to carry it for any length of time.

She went on to look at Bob and thanked him for being kind enough to let her audit the box. She made the point that her cheap plastic box, and its cheap contents could be held up by one finger.

"Can you do that with yours," she asked?

Bob gave a small chuckle and suggested they all drop the box competition and that he was thinking of getting his team a green plastic box.

Alex had realized that the Chief had been standing in the door to his office, watching the exchange among the three of them.

Now at two thirty in the morning, Alex was carrying her light blue box to her first crime scene. She was pleased with her decision of making her box as light as possible.

When she got close to the yellow barrier tape, the scene of the body on the walkway stopped her in her tracks.

She heard Trey quietly mumble that he had come to Cincinnati hoping to get away from the crazies.

The scene of a dead male with his penis pierced by a pencil pinning it up on his stomach and pointing to his belly button took her breath.

She put her poker face on, and recovered her composure, but her eyes were glued to the scene.

She looked around and noticed that all the police members were similarly distracted by the scene.

She approached the body as the medical examiner began his field examination. She asked if he had determined the time of the killing and got the answer that it had most likely been around nine in the evening on the previous day.

She went on to ask the cause of death and was surprised that the pencil was probably the weapon.

The coroner pointed to the blood dripping from the ear.

Alex was surprised to see so little blood but as she looked closer, she noticed that a cotton swab had been pushed into the ear. This was a surprise. It meant the killer had carefully planned and prepared for the kill. It also told her that the killer had not wanted to get blood on himself.

Alex counted out the paces as she walked toward the stadium to the where the yellow tape was placed. She then walked toward the Roebling Bridge to the boundary of the other yellow tape. She then walked out on the grass to the limit of the tape.

Then she walked toward the river. She realized that the distance to the wall was half as far as the other three distances.

She stopped for a moment to speak to the two officers who had been the first on the scene. She complemented them on tapping off the area but inquired why they had not taped off the area toward the river. They responded that they thought the wall made a good barrier to keep people away from the body. She nodded and thanked them again as she went to the wall.

She leaned out toward the river and looked on the ground on the other side of the wall. It was hard to see anything, the lights from the other side of the river and the lights in the park gave enough light for her to know that there seemed to be quite a lot of stuff on the ground. But it was all in the shadows and impossible to distinguish what the articles might be.

She looked over at Trey and realized that he had not moved. She called out to him and watched him react as if he had been sleeping. She knew she would have to address his behavior. She needed his full attention.

She asked him for some gloves and a flashlight. He responded immediately and got gloves and a flashlight for himself as well.

Alex stayed on the park side of the wall. She asked Trey to go to the river side.

The beam of her powerful flashlight was narrow, and the pencil tucked in a crack near the base of the wall made its appearance like an eel in the dark crack of a coral reef.

Once again, Alex stopped breathing as she slowly played the light over the pencil. She quietly called out to Trey. He followed her beam and carefully reached his gloved hand to retrieve the pencil. He picked it up and placed it into the evidence bag that Alex was holding open.

"Thank you, Bill, for making sure I was ready," flashed thorough her mind.

Alex turned and beckoned to the two officers that had taped up the area. She pointed to the pencil and the river side of the wall and asked them to extend the taped area out on the other side of the wall and to arrange the retrieval of all the material that might be evidence on the river side.

Alex carried the pencil to the body and compared it to the one that was in prominent display. The examiner informed her that the blood on the pencil was from a wound in the ear. He went on to say that an autopsy would most likely confirm his belief that the pencil that had been driven into the ear was the cause of death. The pencil through the penis was then staged.

She asked the coroner if she could have the pencil that was on the body and was told to pick it up later after he had a chance to examine how it had been driven in. He went on to make the point that it was difficult to use a pencil in the manner that it had been used and that the ear canal was a very hard target to hit so precisely and driving a pencil through flesh took a fair amount of force.

He wanted to test how much force it took.

Alex thanked him. She stopped and made notes in the black note pad that she picked up from her blue crime scene box. When she was done, she signaled to Trey that it was time to get back to the station.

As they walked to the car, she realized that it was a little after five in the morning and the day had not yet found light. She decided that they should stop for breakfast. It would provide her the opportunity to talk to Trey in a safe, non-threatening environment.

She had decided to ask him about the stress he had talked about before and what effects it was having on him. She needed a full-time, sharp partner.

The coffee shop she selected was a typical, narrow room with a weather-beaten bar, edged by a row of tall chairs on the right-hand side, and a row of dingy brown fake leather covered booths lining the left-hand wall. The wallpaper seams were parting, and some joints had the paper pulled off. The row of tables in the middle, if populated would make the place almost impossible to navigate.

Currently there was only one person at the breakfast bar.

Alex led the way to the table that was situated in the corner just past the last booth.

She sat down and watched as the person behind the bar walked out from behind it and toward them. She could not tell what gender he was and when he asked her for their order his voice did not clear the gender question.

She asked for two eggs over easy, a banana, and a cup of tea.

Trey went for pancakes, two eggs over easy and some bacon. He went for a cup of coffee.

Alex asked about Trey's family. She knew he was married and had a young son, but she really did not know much beyond that.

She listened carefully and asked simple family directed questions. Trey said he had no pictures on him. He explained that it was a precaution on his part. He did not want some bad guy getting his wallet and finding out about his family.

He confided that his driver's license in the wallet was a fake with a fake name. His real drivers license was under his shoe insert.

The precautions that Trey was taking made good sense to Alex.

She asked about his time in Minneapolis and got a brief description of his time on the force there. She learned that his wife and he had been high school sweethearts but had attended separate high schools.

Their connection was skate boarding. They had met in the Mall of America one weekend when they both were boarding the mall.

On his return from Iraq, they got married.

When Alex asked about his experience in Iraq, the conversation came to an end.

Trey said that might be a later conversation.

Alex then took a sip of her tea and asked the question that she knew would most likely not be answered. Not too long ago, she had been in the shoes that she thought Trey was walking in. She had been asked this question by a caring police officer.

The officer had been asked the same question and it eventually led him to change his behavior and take charge of his life.

She asked Trey if he was tired of drinking too much.

Trey looked at her and replied that it was none of her business.

That had been her the response the first time she had been asked. It confirmed what she had suspected. She knew she would ask that question again and she hoped one day Trey would take the action she had taken.

When they got back to the office, she asked Trey to write up the case report. She wanted to get the evidence to the forensics lab and see if the pencil might have fingerprints on it.

She stopped by the morgue to see if she could have the other pencil.

The coroner asked if Alex had found a brick or a stone at the crime scene. He had determined that it would have taken someone hitting the pencil with a hammer or some heavy object to drive the pencil through that penis.

Alex replied that she would go back to the scene and look for any object that could have been used.

She took the pencils to the lab and asked how long it would take to get them examined for fingerprints. She was disappointed that it usually took two or three days.

She let the lab technician know that the pencils were connected to the body found at the River Front Park. This information elucidated the response that the examination for fingerprints would be put on the fast track. It would probably be ready by late in the day.

Alex had been taught her first important lesson, pencils were not a priority, but murder weapons were. She thanked the lab tech and offered to buy her a cup of coffee. When she got the reply that the coffee was free, Alex replied that on her salary it was all she could afford.

3 Fishing

*L*ake Michigan's clear blue waters appeared as a placid, smooth mirror that reflected the early morning sun. He was alone in what he now considered his "old" fishing boat. This was the boat he had purchased when he and Rose-Anne were just recovering from their financial bottom. He bought it because he wanted he, his wife, and their daughter to go out and enjoy fishing together.

He knew that they had been fortunate in finding a great location to live. He had just been elevated to a full professor position at Northwestern. Rose-Anne worked in a prestigious law firm and made at least three times the salary that he brought home.

During a divorce proceeding, she learned of the availability of the home they had finally acquired. Rose-Anne had negotiated with the owner and convinced him to be the title holder.

He had wanted to deny his wife the home and decided to sell it. Rose Anne had made him a very low offer but one that at that time would have been beyond any loan that any mortgage company or bank would have given the two of them.

He sold it to Rose-Anne and did not require a down payment. They moved into a house that was by any measure exclusive and well beyond what he ever imagined he would own.

Their move into the house coincided with Rose-Anne's pregnancy.

A personal promotion at Northwestern, the acquisition of a mansion in an exclusive neighborhood, the arrival of an adorable baby daughter were all events that seemed to him to be too good to be true.

It had taken him years to become accustom to his dream life. His roots were in the poor district of Chicago where gang violence was the rule.

Rose Anne was also from Chicago but had grown up as a Great Lakes "beach girl." She came from a solid middle-class family.

The two of them were from opposite ends of the cultural and financial life experiences.

He loved the lake she loved the shore.

He would often comment that it was a miracle that they loved each other.

They were two poles of a magnet.

Their mutual masterpiece was their daughter. She was smart, head strong, and adventurous. She excelled in school. Made friends easily and seemed to always be in control.

He had bought his "old" boat when Alex turned five. It was the beginning of a father-daughter relationship that brought joy to his heart and today tears to his eyes. Her growth and development had been far too fast for him.

He was sitting by himself in the spot where the two of them had fished every warm weather Saturday for some twenty years.

Fishing had been a daughter and dad event for them since she was five. How he wished it were still so, but time waited on no one and always went forward.

Alex loved to fish, and the fish seemed to gravitate to her pole.

It seemed that ten minutes after arrival and almost every time She would catch a fish. She had always out fished him. She was almost pulled in when a ten-pound trout, one of the biggest either of them had ever caught, hit her line, and took off. He had instinctively grabbed her shoulders and held her in the boat.

He offered to reel in the fish, but she said she was going to do it.

She was way ahead in the number of fish they had caught, and she always brought them to the side of the boat on her own.

The boat was one of the best buys he had ever made. Spending Saturday mornings out on the lake with her was the highlight of every fair-weather weekend.

Sunday was family at church followed by either a picnic in the park or a grill out by the pool at home.

Rose-Anne did not like to eat out but enjoyed cooking for the family and preparing great picnic baskets.

The house the three of them lived in was gull winged in lay out. Gull winged because the center of the house was where the large family room was located. The wings of the house swept forward and around a circular driveway.

A grand entrance foyer with circular steps on each side seemed to embrace the chandelier hanging above a black mahogany circular chest. A tunnel like passageway opened into the family room.

The eyes of a person stepping into the foyer had them guided through the telescope like hallway to the giant fireplace in the family room.

To the left of the foyer was a sitting room and to the right was the dining room that had a grand view of a kitchen made for a Chef.

The right-hand wing had the kitchen and a three-car garage.

Two large bedrooms were on the right wing's second floor. One of the bedrooms was Alex's and the other was her playroom and later her study area.

The left wing of the of the house had the master bedroom, a huge library, an exercise room, a steam bath, a sauna, and a, he and she walk in closet.

The second floor had two additional bedrooms. These remain mostly unused but were outfitted to receive guests.

The pool and grill areas were to the right of the family room.

The house was huge.

Both he and Rose-Anne agreed it was too large of a home for three people but there was no way they would ever give it up.

The fishing pole in his hand brought him out of his daydreaming as a fish hit the line. He gave a small laugh when he realized whose pole he was using. He had spent the first hour using his own pole but did not even have a nibble. He had switched to Alex's pole in hopes of catching something.

He had caught one!

As he unhooked the fish, he thought back about Alex's up bringing.

At school she had at first been harassed because of the color of her skin. She ignored most of the harassment, but she soon put all the bullies in their place. She was willing to be physical in a manner that the bullies understood, and she was fearless. They stop their bullying.

She became the editor of the school newspaper, a stage star in many plays and the top student in her class.

In her senior year she received acceptance letters from Harvard, Dartmouth, and letters from some fourteen states offering her scholarships and other incentives.

He was proud of her when she chose Northwestern. When asked about her choice, she explained that it would be free to her, and she could continue to cook and fish with her favorite Mom and Dad.

Everyone had a good laugh when Rose-Anne asked about her other less favorite parents.

Rose-Anne had often expressed the fact that Alex preferred dad over mom. This of course he knew was not true. Rose-Anne and Alex had spent many hours cooking together. They had also taken up knitting for some time. They were very close.

When Alex pursued the law field, he teased Rose-Anne about being the favorite.

Rose-Anne was overjoyed when Alex joined a Chicago law firm.

Six months later Alex accepted a position as a deputy sheriff in the small community of Zion, Illinois.

Rose-Ann was mad as h---. She saw the move as a step down and found it hard to understand.

He understood and knew that office life was not for Alex. She was an outside kind of person and needed movement and action.

When confronted, Alex's simple answer was that her mom thrived and loved being a prosecutor.

She, on the other hand, could not stand being cooped up in an office. She wanted to be as good as her mother but in the field finding the bad guys that she could bring to the prosecutor.

She was going fishing for the bad guys and her mother could fillet and cook them.

This had defused the situation.

He gazed across the calm lake waters. It was now close to eleven in the morning. He placed the large trout he had caught into the holding tank. It was large enough for a family of four and would make at least two meals for he and Rose-Anne.

The motor purred as he turned the key, and he aimed the bow toward the distant Church Steeple.

He smiled at the good memories and wondered how Alex was doing in her new role as a Cincinnati detective. It made him feel good knowing she was doing what she loved.

3 Fishing

4 *Trey's Return to Normal*

Return to normal was difficult. Trey knew his experience in Iraq had messed with his mind. He availed himself to the help the Marine Corps offered him, but his periodic flash backs often caught him off guard. He had lost several of his platoon in a fire fight and then his armored vehicle hit an IED. He received a Purple Heart and a Navy and Marine Combat Action Ribbon.

The loss of his brother's in arms overshadowed any recommendation they could give him.

On his return to Minneapolis, he retraced his younger life and being a mall rate in the Mall of America. It was the place where he had perfected his skateboarding skills and had met the person that was now his wife.

He had met Lindsey on one of those skateboarding outings. She was not only overwhelmingly beautiful with her blond hair blown back as she navigated her board down the steps, took the railing, and swooshed to a stop at the bottom to greet him but her blue eyes froze him on the spot. On that first meeting he had not been able to say a word.

She smiled at him and asked if he was good enough to keep up with her. He had kept up. He fell in love that day. She later let him know that she had him in her sites much earlier than their first meeting.

Meeting and falling in love with Lindsey changed him. She lifted him both spiritually and mentally.

They went to different schools but met regularly in the Mall.

He graduated high school one year before her. He planned to go to college and had good enough grades to do so but he had no idea what to study.

Instead, he joined the Marine Corps. After boot camp and survival training, he was assigned to a unit that ended up in Iraq.

Lindsey's picture and their mutual correspondence had carried him through his tour of Iraq.

Iraq changed him but he was determined to make something of himself. He wanted to get well and move on with his life.

Lindsey made it clear that she unconditionally supported him and wanted to be involved in his recovery. She went with him to several sessions with the psychiatrist.

Lindsey was now one class ahead of him at the University of Minnesota. He felt lucky to be in the same University with her.

Their romance flourished and life seemed to get back to normal.

Waking up in a cold sweat happened often and he continued to see the psychiatrist. He felt he was making strides in becoming a normal guy.

He proposed marriage and they had a small family wedding in their second year. They had their parents and invited a few friends and had the ceremony in the University chapel.

When he graduated, he accepted a job as a detective in the Minneapolis police force. It was a huge department, and it was involved in the investigation of many shootings and killings.

It was not the stress of combat, but the assault was from the very people that he was sworn to protect.

He was soon drinking.

Lindsey begged him to stop, and he would do so for a short time.

Then the pressure overwhelmed him, and he was back to drinking.

The birth of a son, Nolan, caused him to be more disciplined and he put the bottle away.

He thought he had overcome his addiction.

For several years, he managed the intense stress he felt when he was investigating a murder or facing a risky situation.

Just after Nolan's fifth birthday, a boy of the same age was kidnapped and later found in dead in a lake outside of the city.

He and his partner were assigned to the case.

They successfully hunted the killer down but during the arrest the kidnapper killed his partner.

This pushed Trey over the edge and once again he took up the bottle.

His return to drinking was a signal that he needed to change jobs.

A job posting looking for a detective in Cincinnati seemed to be what he was looking for. He figured a smaller city meant a lower crime rate and fewer killings.

Lindsey agreed with him, and he contacted the Cincinnati Chief of Detectives and did an interview over the phone.

He was elated to get the job and accepted being a partner with a female detective as the lead. This part had been a condition of his employment. It was a condition he welcomed.

He was sure a small sleepy city like Cincinnati would present him with a lot less stress than he was currently experiencing. Later to his dismay he learned that Cincinnati had the third per capita rate of crime and killing in the nation.

It was a deadly, sleepy town!

His entrance interview when he arrived in Cincinnati with Chief Johnson went well. He took an instant liking to the Chief and his direct manner. The Chief was impressed with the fact that he had distinguished himself and had received the Navy and Marine Combat Action Ribbon for his bravery.

Trey responded positively when the Chief inquired about being in the support role to a black female detective. To Trey, neither color, nor gender had ever been an issue. He was first a Marine, now a detective and he was confident and sure of himself.

He stood up when Alex, his new partner walked through the door, shook her hand, and stated that he was pleased to meet her. He knew the only problem he might have would be when Lindsey saw the beautiful black woman that was his work partner.

It was not quite the same as when he had first met Lindsey, but Alex's eyes froze him to the spot, and he could not let go of her hand.

She smiled and relaxed her hand and replied that she too was very pleased to meet him and to have him as her work partner.

The Chief broke the spell by asking them both to sit down.

He said he wanted them to be a successful team but that the odds were stacked against them. The chief of police had been against having a female leading a detective team.

He added that the Chief of Police had also been against him becoming Chief of Detectives.

He added that the Chief of Police was not a supporter of the department.

He wanted to interview each of you. I told him not until the two of you have a few cases under your belts. I don't need his approval to run my department.

I want to meet with you once a week for the next couple of months, then we will meet less often. I suggest the two of you get to know each other well and learn how to work smoothly together. This is not school but there are plenty of bullies on the force that will try to get your goat. Deal with it.

Trey watched as Alex looked at the Chief and beamed a smile that transfixed him and simply replied that bullies had been her specialty all her life. She looked at Trey and continued to say that now that she had an experienced Marine hero with several years of street experience as a partner, her team was the best in the unit. She went on to say that at this point it was only talk, but very soon she and Trey would demonstrate their teamwork power.

Trey looked at Alex, nodded and quietly said, "Hurrah." He was certain he had made the right decision. He had her back.

A couple of months followed where he concentrated on moving into his new home. He and Lindsey had decided to rent until they had time to better understand the Cincinnati area and the places available for them to move into or where they might build a new home. Given their income and the expense of moving, building a new home was probably not an option at the current time.

Together they decided that it would be better if he concentrated on getting into his work cycle while they took their time to find the right home.

It turned out that the workload was at a low ebb. He and Alex focused on getting to know each other better and in unity fend off the workplace obstacles put before them by several people.

One of those persons sat in the desk behind Trey. Alex had positioned her desk so she could face Trevor and his partner Bill.

Trey quietly observed the manner that Alex fended off and usually got the better of the exchanges passed between her and

Trevor. It was clear to Trey that his work partner had a tough demeaner and easily held her own in the rough work area give and take. Her smile never left her face. Trey resolved never to play poker with her.

The two in the morning call to action caught Trey at the wrong time. He had fallen off the wagon and had gone to sleep late. Lindsey had to shake him repeatedly before he came awake. She asked if she should tell the dispatcher that he was sick.

Trey knew he had screwed up at the wrong time. He took a quick cold shower and then threw on his clothes and went to the office.

He walked into the bull pen area and saw that Alex was ready to go. She pointed to a cup of coffee and waved for him to follow her.

He grabbed the coffee and followed Alex to their old car.

There was utter silence on the short drive to the riverfront. Trey was not sure how to interpret Alex's behavior.

He was having trouble staying awake and decided to concentrate on doing so.

When they got to the crime scene, Trey was shocked. He had never seen such a depraved killing. He wondered about his decision of moving to Cincinnati.

He didn't realize he had frozen on the spot until he heard Alex calling to him.

"Damn, he thought to himself, "Our first meaningful case and I am a wreck and barely able to function."

He could not let this happen again.

5 *The Chief*

Bruce knew that he had been put in place as a trial. He was the first black Chief of Detectives. The City had put pressure on the police department to get their force integrated and diverse. Doing so meant keeping the federal government out. The current Chief of Police had complied but was a lukewarm supporter of integration.

Bruce was from Mississippi and knew the face of discrimination and the Chief of Police, though he always said he was for integration was in fact a closet supporter of white is better. Not fully racist but not color blind. He carried his lifetime of conditioning and experience, and it was a white experience.

Cincinnati was more civil about discrimination. Discrimination was in full bloom, but the flower was worn more politely.

He had recently hired the first black female detective. He had been looking for a black candidate and had to smile when he recognized his own life's experience at discrimination because he was thinking about hiring a black "male" detective during his search.

He was impressed with her ability to be in command of the situation. She was black but had enjoyed all the privileges of an upper-middle-class white upbringing. Her education was solid. She had clerked for a judge in Chicago but then had chosen to become a policewoman in the small town of Zion, Illinois. The sheriff of Zion had told him she was the smartest person that had ever worked for him, and she was tough as they came. The sheriff made the point he was white and that she had taught him what it meant to recognize his own racial bias. He went on to say that he considered her a good friend.

Bruce had hired her immediately. So far, she had been exactly what he had hoped for. The fact that his wife had immediately liked her and now asked every day how she was doing reassured him. His wife was an astute reader of character. She had vetted every one of his detectives. He had reassigned several detectives based on her recommendation. So far, she was batting one thousand.

When he had made the decision to hire her, he had checked more deeply into her family.

He was impressed with the fact that her father was a full professor at Northwestern and that her mother was a well-known prosecutor who was somewhat of a heroine. She provided pro-bono services to the black community and had a huge following base on her support in the black community.

He hoped that Alex's character seed had fallen close to her mother's tree.

He had watched her spar with Trevor and to bring Bob into her fold. Trevor was a top detective but always chose to tease or harass certain people. It seemed he had singled out Alex for his harassment. He was losing. The Chief hoped that Trevor would recognize that he was out of his league and stop harassing Alex.

After watching Trevor and Alex spar, it was clear Alex had the high road and the upper hand.

This morning, he had come in early and was about to head to the crime scene at the River Front Park when Alex and Trey walked in. He observed the two and took in the fact that Alex did not invite Trey to come into his office with her. Usually, teams came to him together.

He looked again at Trey and wondered if he were sick. He did not look good.

Alex's steady approach gave him pause. She seemed mad about something but when she walked into the office her beaming smile wiped away the thought brewing in his head.

Alex held up two evidence bags. Each sealed evidence bag had a pencil inside. He listened as Alex held up the bag with a bloody pencil. She quietly said, "This is the murder weapon and the pencil that was driven through the victim's penis to hold it pointing it to his belly button. It was first driven into his ear canal and into his brain. It is the kill weapon.

She then held up the bag with a second pencil that seemed to be a duplicate of the first, but it did not have any blood on it. She explained that she had found the second pencil in a crack on the river side, at the base of the stone wall. But it had no blood on it. She figured the killer may have dropped it and not been able to retrieve it.

She described the crime scene and conjectured that the assailant was a woman. She quickly retracked her last statement and said that it was her gut reaction to the scene, and she had no basis for voicing her reaction.

He was pleased with Alex's demeaner. He asked what her next step would be and was pleased to hear that she was on the way to the lab to see if there were any fingerprints or DNA on the pencils.

She said she stopped to get him up to speed because she felt he needed to be in the driver's seat. The location and the nature of the killing would leak, and she figured he was about to be in the hot seat.

She went on to say that she had his back.

His phone rang and he gave Alex the signal for her to go.

It was his boss. He had heard about the murder and wanted reassurance that the best detectives were on the case.

Bruce smiled. Alex had just demonstrated that she was among the best. She had indeed gotten him ready for the hot seat.

Bruce replied that he had the best on the case and wouldn't have it any other way and that as soon as he had any useful information, he would give him a call.

Bruce knew he would get a call as soon as his boss figured out that Alex was the person assigned to the murder case. He hoped that by the time the political waters got muddy, Alex would have the case resolved.

He went over to Trey's desk and saw that he was writing out a report about the case. There were about a dozen pictures and a small black book with notes that Trey was typing into the computer.

Bruce expressed his interest in getting the report as quickly as possible. He shared that his boss was already inquiring about the River Front case.

Trey looked up and replied that it would be on his desk within the hour after Alex reviewed it and put in what she had learned from the coroner and the fingerprint lab.

Trevor and Bob were just walking into the bull pen. Bruce signaled for them to come into his office.

He wanted to make sure the two of them pitched in to help in solving the case, but he wanted them to support not lead. It was a little different than the usual arrangement. Bill and Trevor were normally in the lead with other teams supporting them.

He watched the two as he shared what he knew about the River Front homicide. Bill just nodded but Trevor raised an objection about playing second fiddle to a new team that had no lead experience or solved one crime in Cincinnati.

He responded that Trevor was right, but he was asking for them to support. If that was unacceptable, he would get another team to provide backup support. That was when Bill spoke up and said that they would provide whatever backup, Alex requested. He went on to say that in the future he would expect Alex's support if they needed it.

Bruce understood Trevor's attitude and he recognized why Bill was the team leader. He assured them that it would always be his expectation that teams helped each other when needed.

He thanked them and told them there was nothing to do immediately but he had wanted to have this discussion before their support was needed.

Once they were out of the room. He placed a call to the mayor to update him on the case and that the best resources of the unit were being put on the case.

6 The River Front Runner

Greg was unaware that an upcoming decision would be the most important one in his life. His mind was on the love of his life, and she overshadowed any other thoughts.

He had taken the day off because Samantha's birthday fell on a Thursday. He had not mentioned his day off to her. He wanted to make her birthday celebration a total surprise.

Samantha had gone to work at the twin tower building where they both worked.

He had spent the day preparing a special dinner for Samantha. He hoped it would be a big hit.

He had looked up the recipe for Spaghetti de Mare earlier in the week and had shopped for all the ingredients. He included making a mixed salad with romaine lettuce, tomato slices and chopped cucumber. He topped it with an olive oil and vinegar dressing. A loaf of garlic-buttered Italian bread rounded out the dinner.

He looked at his accomplishment with a great deal of pride.

The wine was a chilled bottle of Moscato d'Asti.

After dinner he planned to play being the Italian barista and served a smooth cup of Cappuccino that was foam covered and sweet. He had practiced making the foam into the shape of a heart.

He had met Samantha during a financial audit of the plant he had managed. They dated for almost a year then just prior to learning he was being promoted, they married. It was one of the happiest days of his life.

Samantha loved her career and made a point that she was not going to be a typical "housewife."

Greg loved to cook, and he had always been a "keep it clean freak." It was easy for him to accept that they would both be work hounds and would both share equally in keeping their outside of work load balanced.

On learning that he would be promoted and would need to relocate to Cincinnati, he and Samantha had agreed that they should buy a house. They had found one in Price Hill within walking distance of work, but it needed massive renovation. They chose to rent a water front apartment because it was within walking distance to their twin tower offices, and it would let them evaluate whether walking to work from their new home would be realistic.

The apartment was near the Ohio river and the almost five-mile-long riverside running trail. It allowed him to continue his training for what was going to be his first marathon. He planned to begin his marathon running by participating in Cincinnati's own Flying Pig Marathon.

His goal was to compete in as many marathons as he could and then be accepted to run in what he thought of as the "premier" of marathons, "The Boston Marathon."

That evening, seeing Samantha's surprised look when she walked in and saw the candles, the wine and the large salad on the table was the only reward he needed. He of course did not turn down her hug and kiss. Her "you shouldn't have," and "how did you get all this ready,," and the "I love you," certainly made him feel great. He twirled her around. She put her briefcase down and he guided her to the table.

He was sure he was enjoying the evening more than her.

He insisted on cleaning the kitchen and that she take a shower and then together they would finish the wine.

The rest of the evening flowed smoothly and was a night to be remembered.

They both worked on Friday.

After work they agreed on an early, simple dinner and threw a small pizza in the oven. Greg was OK with the pizza since after dinner he planned to run at least ten miles and the pasta would be quickly consumed.

Shortly after dinner he left the apartment. It was a little later than he intended but he felt great as he turned up-river. His starting point was the Serpentine Wall. He turned up-river and went past the Purple People Bridge. He noted that Yeatman's Cove had a few people walking but no concert.

As always, the traffic across the Daniel Carter Beard Bridge was steady but the rush hour was over. As he went past the Montgomery Inn several people in the parking lot shouted encouragement.

He was pacing himself at the speed that he planned to run for the first half of the marathon. The air was coming at him from the front and his hair was being swept back. It made him feel like a fast runner, but he knew he was not among the elite first-class runners. He concentrated on his breathing, but all the while his eyes took in the surroundings.

The sun descending behind him made it look as if his shadow was out running him. He felt like speeding up to overtake it and laughed at his animal like response.

He felt good.

To the right the river seemed a little muddy and seemed to have more logs floating by than he expected but he recalled it had rained the day before, so he figured the runoff had brought extra debris into the river.

At the end of the trail, he turned around.

The sun's last rays were fighting with the horizon and would soon be gone.

He was now on the downtown portion of the run where the river front lighting illuminated the trail. He passed the apartment and continued under the Taylor bridge and the public landing where he ran on the sidewalk until he reached the new Smale Riverfront Park then he ran along the river side walkway and went through the tunnel under the Roebling suspension bridge.

Since it was now dark and a Thursday, he was not surprised to find the park empty. He ran past the Smale Park area and took a loop around Paul Brown stadium and headed back to the apartment building.

He got to the it and stopped in front of it. This was his decision point. He had run almost 10 miles. He often chose to stop at that distance, but he wanted to get ready to fly a lot better than a pig. This time he felt great and decided to repeat the run to the stadium and back. His decision was based on his mood and how he felt physically. He usually did it again. It put him closer to having run fifteen miles. This was the ideal distance to prepare for a marathon run and he wanted to be ready.

He was feeling good and decided to pick up the pace slightly. He was soon running around the Paul Brown stadium and was on his return.

Up ahead he saw a person standing in front of what appeared to be an artist's easel. He wondered what the artist was planning to paint at this time in the evening. It was dark except for the lights from the buildings on the Kentucky side of the river.

Greg thought the lights were indeed captivating. He wondered if that was what the artist was trying to capture.

He was just getting ready to look at the easel when the artist stepped directly in front of him. He hit her in full stride and almost knocked her down, but his quick reflexes let him hold her up.

He began to apologize for having hit her.

She smiled at him, thanked him for catching her and asked him to take a look at her easel.

He took a step toward the easel to take a look. The artist's movement caused him to turn, and he tried to step away from her. Then he felt a piercing pain.

His last thought was of Samantha, then a bright light and finally the world went black.

7 The Perfect crime

Dianne got up early. She took her time preparing a healthy breakfast. Before she sat down, she took her waterfront sketch and placed it on the easel in her painting bedroom. She had taken the time to sketch in the scene at the river front. In the next few days, she would paint it and create her first in a series that she planned to call, Runner's Revenge," she planned to make the series a long one.

She sat in the breezeway that was directly behind the kitchen area with the tv on and her two boiled eggs that she had "decapitated" with her egg decapper. She was eager to see what the morning news would have to report.

She flipped to her favorite station. It began with her favorite line, "Breaking News." Of course, in Cincinnati, any news was breaking news. The news report was highlighting the police investigation of her first kill.

She was very curious about what the police was up to, but she was not worried about them. She had been very careful to make sure she had not left any fingerprints and she had used gloves to make sure she did not leave any DNA. She had wiped down the victim's hands to make sure he had not gotten anything on them from her during the collision.

The police would have nothing to investigate.

She wondered about her victim's name and what he did. She figured that the news would soon disclose that information.

She was betting on the person working and living in the downtown area. She thought he would be some kind of professional. She figured he was probably a jerk and that she most likely had done someone a favor in picking him.

The report other than stating that a person had been killed in the new section of the park had no detail other than the fact that there would be a police news update later in the morning.

She looked at the clock and decided she would have just enough time to put on the base coating for her new painting. She liked to paint a thin coating over her sketch to seal the canvas but allowed the sketch to be seen. This would set it up so when she came home from work, she could begin painting.

During the drive to work she brooded over the injustices that had happened to her. She went through a list.

She had been seriously injured by a careless runner and then denied her day in court.

She should have landed a position in a much more prestigious museum but for some reason that had not come to pass.

At this museum she should already be in charge. She was brilliant at her curator's job but had an incompetent boss that should have been fired.

If the roles were reversed, she would fire him.

She would have chosen him as her first kill, but she had not figured out the scenario where she would not get caught. She would take him out if she ever had the chance.

She stopped her listing when a car honked repeatedly, and she realized the light was green.

She focused on getting to work.

Getting to her office was a major accomplishment. She had returned from the Chicago Marathon and was bound to a wheelchair. She no longer needed it, but she had learned to leverage it.

Getting a parking spot thirty feet from the elevator was one privilege she liked.

She unloaded the chair, sat down and then wheeled it toward the entrance.

The guard, Jake, held the door open and she rolled effortlessly to the elevator.

She rolled in and went behind her desk.

This morning, she was thinking about her next victim and what his background might be.

Her thoughts were interrupted when her boss gave a brief knock and then walked through the door. He wanted to meet with her about a traveling art collection that would be arriving in a few weeks. The museum would hold several viewings of the collection that needed planning. The layout of the art exhibits was another point he wanted to discuss.

Dianne smiled and replied she would be pleased to do the planning, the layout, and the advertising for the art viewing.

This was the part of her job she loved.

The timing of the art collection arrival was opportune. She would plan the timing and set up several evening agendas that would provide the window that she could utilize to provide her with an alibi. Her attitude improved and the coming work was not as heavy of a burden as she had worried it might be.

The realization that her current job would consistently provide the means to have an alibi whenever an art showing was scheduled made her smile and feel a warm surge of pleasure. The future looked bright. She could begin enjoying the Cincinnati area and all the culture and entertainment it offered and carry out her runner's revenge at the same time.

She went down to the coffee shop for a cup of coffee and decided that a morning blueberry muffin would make a good add.

Once back in her office, she tuned into channel five to see if they had anything to report. They had an update to the killing.

She held her cup of coffee in both hands and listened.

The police had not determined a motive and they were seeking the public's assistance in identifying any potential suspects.

Dianne smiled, clueless, the cops were clueless. She had pulled off the perfect crime. She would soon add another to her accomplishments. She was a little saddened that her target was a P&G employee and that he was married. She would have preferred a dirty, twice divorced lawyer. She figured most of them were crooks.

Dianne nibbled on her blueberry muffin and contemplated the timing of her next victim. She wished she could get the names of her targets to make sure she was not somehow being biased in her selection. She figured fair was fair but there was no way that she could know that ahead of time.

She shook her head at the thought and let out an almost silent cackle.

She laughed again as she thought about how clueless the police were about her first kill.

Part of the upcoming art exhibit was some pottery. She decided to have a similar contest to the one she had done with sketching. She could set up ten pottery wheels and have the clay ready for use. The pots made by the patrons would go to the art school for finishing and then could be purchased in the form of donations. She was sure she would be able to raise several thousand dollars for the museum and probably more for the schools.

During the pottery contest, she could slip out and carry out her killing and return before anyone noticed.

She saw it as a win-win-win situation.

She hummed as she went about developing the agenda.

She knew she was blessed.

She decided to go downtown and have lunch. She usually did not go out because it took extra effort to do so but she just had to celebrate her first success.

She stayed to character and used her wheelchair.

The sky was a deep blue and a few puffy white popcorn clouds floated slowly across over the buildings. They were playing hide and seek behind the taller buildings.

If she were walking, her way through the park would have given her a view of the river. She really would have loved to take a stroll along the river to where she had set up her easel. It would have made the lunch outing much more memorable. Her recent accomplishment would have been icing on the cake; so sweet to her taste.

Just from the thought, she seemed to gain new energy.

The church bells seemed to confirm her righteous emotions.

The trip to and from the steak house made the total lunch time longer than planned but she figured that she deserved it.

She wheeled herself slowly back to the museum and decided that she would take the afternoon off and go to Eden park. She would use the time to decide on the best location for her next adventure.

When she got back to her office, she began to put away the work she had been doing.

She was just getting ready to turn on the news to see if there was any more information about her riverfront masterpiece when a young woman followed by a more grizzled male stood in the door and asked if she had a few moments. The woman then flashed a badge and the man standing behind her did the same.

Dianne was surprised. She wondered how they had come to be at her door.

What had she missed?

She invited them in and asked to take a closer look at their badges. This allowed her time to recover and to get the names on the badges.

She read the names out loud, "Alex Evercrest and Trey McGregor."

"Nice names, how may I help you?"

She had no intentions of helping but she was eager to find out what they might know.

8 The Pencils

Alex pulled out the pencil she had found on the riverside of the stone wall. From a partial fingerprint and a very thorough technician searching various data bases, she had learned that the name of the person behind the desk was Dianne. Dianne had a spotless record. She was only in a fingerprint data base because she was fingerprinted when she went to work for the museum.

Alex asked her if the pencil was hers.

Dianne examined the pencil and said it looked a lot like the pencils she used and asked where it had been found.

She was surprised that the pencil had so quickly been tracked to her and asked about it. She went on to say that over the course of the last year she had probably lost a dozen pencils along the riverfront, but this was the first time any of them had found the way back home.

Alex had been watching closely to see if there would be any hesitation or other indication that Dianne was lying. To Alex the answer was too smooth. She knew immediately she was talking to a superb liar.

She was about to challenge Dianne with a more pointed question when the phone rang.

Dianne excused herself and mouthed the word, "Boss." As she turned to answer, it became obvious that she was sitting in a wheelchair.

This was Dianne's intention.

Alex looked over to Trey who nodded and shrugged his shoulders.

Dianne agreed to a meeting time and then turned back to the two detectives.

She logged the call as a call from God.

It had given her the opportunity to make the fact that she was in a wheelchair glaringly obvious.

She was now waiting to see what the two would do.

Alex was not convinced. Her senses were saying that she was looking at the murderer, but the facts seemed to contradict her gut.

She asked the obvious question.

I'm sorry to see that you are in a wheelchair, how did that happen?

Dianne replied that she had broken her hip and was getting physical therapy in hopes that she would walk again. She watched to see if that would have the effect of diffusing the suspicion of her being the killer. She could not tell by the expression on the female detective's face.

She tried to remember her name but came up blank. The look on the other detective told her that he had taken her off the suspect list.

Alex thanked Dianne for her time and told her she might come back at a later time.

Alex exited from her interview in a confused state. The pencil she found on the base of the river wall and the pencil used as the murder weapon were duplicates. They both belonged to the person she still suspected of murder.

The questions that kept repeating in her mind was, how could a person in a wheelchair kill a very healthy long-distance-runner.

And why would she want to kill him?

The evidence did not add up. She had somehow misread the crime scene. She decided that she did not have enough information.

There had been a lot of evidence picked up on the river side of the retaining wall where she had found the second pencil. She needed to find out if there were any other clues in the trash that had been picked up.

Trey was inclined to dismiss Dianne as a suspect. He was sure there would be another clue to be found in the material or perhaps from the park's surveillance cameras.

Alex decided to bring the Chief up to date and see if he had any suggestions on how to proceed.

Before returning to the office, Alex suggested they park straight across from the museum. She told Trey that they were going to see if they could find a way to the park that had no surveillance cameras.

She walked back to the museum and looked around at all the buildings. She found one spot at the top of the driveway leading to the parking behind the museum.

She looked out across the park and found a rotating camera on the building across the street and was able to cross and get behind a statue in the center of the park before it came back around.

She looked ahead and to her right and saw a similar camera that was mounted on the building ahead of her. She walked to the base of the building that had the camera and looked up. She would not be seen.

She continued toward downtown until she came to a street with no cameras in view in either direction. The street led down to the river. She walked to the river and found a way to get to the crime scene without getting seen.

She was now certain that she had just interviewed the killer.

The wheelchair was the one barrier that she had to consider. Coming down to the river would have been possible but going back to the museum or away from the river would have meant going uphill. She would have to find out if the wheelchair was motorized.

Dianna sat for a while thinking through what had just transpired. She had been alarmed by how close and how soon the two detectives had come to finding her.

She decided it would be a good idea to go and have dinner on the square. If they were watching, they would see an invalid struggling to wheel her chair along the city street. They would have to believe it would have been impossible for her to commit the crime.

Alex had not thought about trying to watch what Dianne would do.

On the way back to her car she spotted one surveillance camera she had missed. It was on the corner of the P&G twin towers closest to the river. It was a fixed camera that pointed toward the alley leading from the park toward the building. She walked down the alley and then to the giant entrance doors to the service desk. Soon she was talking to the head of security and was informed that she could have the view from the camera for the day that she had requested. It was all digital and would be sent to the police station computer.

Alex thanked the Chief of security. His response was that she should get the bastard that had killed one of his people.

Alex led the way back to the car. Trey had not spoken a word for the entire walk. When they got back to the car he asked if Alex had figured out how an invalid could kill a robust, strong, and healthy runner.

Alex looked at him and simply said that she would figure it out.

He shrugged his shoulder but said nothing.

Once back in the office she organized her notes and then knocked on the Chief's door. She shared her story and she asked how he thought she should proceed.

The Chief's response was to ask her several questions. He asked her how she would proceed.

Alex replied that she had obtained some security camera footage from a camera on the P&G tower building. She would put in a request to get the camera footage for every camera she had identified. She planned to view all of them to see what would show up. She was waiting for the results of having all the trash examined. She had decided to interview her suspect's boss to see if she could get a better understanding of the work environment and situation.

She finished by stating that a missing person's report coinciding with the murder time frame had been registered and that she was going to interview the person who called in the report.

The Chief looked at her, smiled and said, "I think you have answered your own question about what to do and it sounds like you need to get going."

He then waved her out of his office.

9 Alex's The Mother

*T*he bookcase full of legal references framed the central open section where the treasures in her life were on display. The picture in the center was one taken on Alex's Northwestern Graduation. Alex was in the center with her on the right side and Russel on the other side. This picture was surrounded by other pictures of the three of them at various times in the short period that Alex was growing up.

The week had started out with the news of the killing along the Cincinnati Riverfront.

Rose-Anne got a call from Alex telling her not to worry about the River Front case and that she had a great partner that had her back. She shared that she anticipated a rather dull case of gathering evidence and finally making an arrest.

Before the call she had not connected Alex to the case. Now she was worried. It was hard for her to imagine her daughter trying to apprehend and bring in someone who had demonstrated their brutality and desire to kill.

What also worried her was that Alex would not stop until she was face to face with the killer. Alex had always been hands on and direct.

Against her personal and emotional inclination against fighting, when Alex turned twelve, she had enrolled her into Tae Kwando classes. Alex became a black belt in a few years. Now Rose-Ann hoped Alex had kept up her practice routine. And it helped that she was armed.

When Alex attended Northwestern and excelled in the field of Law, Rose-Ann had been thrilled. When Alex went to work for Judge Lungren, Rose-Ann had been ecstatic.

Then it seemed that almost overnight Alex had thrown away what seemed like a spectacular start to becoming a successful lawyer. She took a job as a common policeman in the sleepy little town of Zion.

Her first reaction was to disown Alex, but Russel had stopped her and recounted how responsible and how thoughtful Alex had been.

She had made sure the family did not get loaded down with college expenses by attending Northwestern where he was a professor, and she got a free ride.

She had gone into the field of law, but she had confided to him that if she could have figured out how to make a living, she would have sought an Art or Music degree.

Rose-Anne knew why she and Russel got along so well. They were polar opposites that loved each other and together had an overwhelming magnetic bond. They each loved their daughter as well.

Now Rose-Ann could see that Alex was on her way to becoming a top detective. She finally understood what Alex's statement that "she planned to be the one that caught the bad guys so prosecutors like her mother could send them to jail," meant.

She thought about all the times she and Alex had cooked together. Alex was a great student. She herself was a registered chef. She had become a chef for her own interest and had never had any intention of being a practicing chef. She recognized Alex as having almost the same cooking skills as she had.

She went to Alex's room and looked at the awards on the wall and the trophies earned in Tae Kwando but what now seemed more significant was all the artworks.

Every piece had a special meaning.

There was the boat out on the lake with two people fishing. Rose-Anne knew it was Russel and Alex. She recognized the outfit that she and Alex had made as a mother-daughter project.

There was the pencil sketch of a courtroom with a person facing the bench. She recognized the judge and the witness. She remembered it was a summer day a few years ago when Alex had come to court with her and had spent her time in the court seats.

There was the drawing of the pool area with a host of friends painted in watercolor. Every person in the painting was recognizable.

It was clear to Rose-Ann that she had a talented daughter that might have done very well had she chosen to be an artist.

Rose-Anne thought back over all the years of raising Alex.

She knew she had sent Alex to a school that had was essentially ninety five percent white.

Still Alex had thrived.

She was a black girl that had grown up white. Alex had excelled in every aspect.

She graduated high school as number one in her class.

She had been the first female editor of the school paper.

She was a varsity field hockey star.

And a stage star in numerous theatrical plays.

Alex had added debate and speaking skills to her resume.

She was more than any mother might have wished for.

Her attendance at Northwestern and participation in a variety of programs was a repeat of her high school achievements.

Russel had bought her a dark green, low, and long, twelve-cylinder Jaguar for her to drive. It was a high school graduation gift that Alex drove for four years to the university.

It was now covered and parked in the garage. Once a week Russel drove it to work. He claimed that in needed to be used to keep it in good shape. Rose-Anne knew he was probably right, but she also knew how much he missed his father-daughter activities.

She was sure he had his own contacts that followed what Alex was doing.

Rose-Anne and Russel had been at the match where Alex progressed to a Third-degree black belt. The black belt cost Alex a broken toe but she won that match when it appeared that her opponent was taken aback that Alex just taped her broken toe to her big toe and proceeded with the match.

The cheer of the event spectators reminded Rose-Anne of the scenes of Nero in the Colosseum in Rome and Alex was the gladiator.

Thinking about the case that Alex was now on, she wished she had encouraged her to go into art. She thought, "the pencil was mightier than the sword," and art was a safer endeavor than being a detective.

She had called one of her old college friends that now was working for WLW in Cincinnati in the newsroom to find out what she could learn.

She learned that it was a bizarre killing on the river front. The bizarre part was that a pencil had been used as the weapon to kill. Then afterwards, the victim who evidently was a runner had been posed with his penis pinned to his abdomen by the pencil that had been used to kill him.

This made her more worried than she anticipated.

She wondered if Alex knew she was dealing with a deranged killer.

Rose-Anne had no doubt about the fearlessness of her daughter and no doubt about her intellect. She was just worried about some crazy killer harming her in an unexpected way.

She knew she had to get over her worry.

She stopped her rumination.

10 The Wife

*A*lex was frustrated by the lack of progress.

The fingerprint that was on the pencil that she found at the base of the riverfront wall had led her to the person she suspected.

The suspect was in a wheelchair.

At best the pencil was circumstantial evidence.

The waste that was picked up on the river side of the wall had yielded a large number of fingerprints that would take forever to process and would not mean much since there were no fingerprints associated with victim of the crime scene.

She did not even know the name of the victim!

The Chief had told her to get to work.

Work on what?

Trey made a comment about not even having a missing person's report.

Alex looked at Trey, pointed to him and rushed out.

She made a beeline to where the reports were reviewed and assigned to be investigation. She knew that calls that came in too early were held until the twenty-four-hour mark. Then a follow up call was done.

She asked about any report that might still not have reached the twenty-four-hour threshold. There was one and when she reviewed it, she knew that from the details of the call that it was the victim's wife who had called to report him missing. She had been given the standard twenty-four hour wait rule.

Alex now had a name. The caller was Samantha; the missing husband was Greg. Greg had left for a jog from his riverside apartment around seven thirty in the evening. According to the coroner Greg was dead forty-five minutes later.

Trey caught up with her as she held the missing person's report in her hand and told him the victim's name was Greg.

She gave Trey a hug and told him he had just earned a free breakfast.

He smiled and asked what he had done to earn it.

She responded by waving the missing person's report.

Alex's elation took a nosedive when she realized she would have to interview the wife.

She had already concluded that the runner was truly just out running and had crossed paths with his killer only because the killer had set a trap.

She had at first wondered if this runner had used running as an excuse for a rendezvous or some other clandestine reason.

She had concluded that it had been fate.

He had been dressed like a runner, not like someone out to meet a lover.

She found it hard to imagine a spurned lover leaving such a lewd imagery.

It was time for her to contact the wife and find out about her river front victim.

She placed a call that went straight to the answering machine. The message gave the wife's work office phone number.

The call to the work number was answered immediately. Alex let Samantha know that she was following up on the missing person's report and ask if she were available to discuss the report.

There was a moment of silence.

Then Samantha suggested they meet at her apartment.

Samantha slowly put what she had been working on neatly into the folders where they belonged. She locked her desk and let her boss know that she was going home for lunch.

She made a stop in the lady's room before going to the elevator. She needed to regain her composure she wondered if the police had any information, and she was worried it was bad news.

She knew, she was sure she knew who the person killed in the park was. Tears ran down her cheek. She was so angry, and she felt swallowed by a black abyss. She dried her eyes and decided to take the freight elevator down to the first floor. She wanted to get out of the building without meeting anyone.

She walked down the alley that she and Greg had walked every day for the last year.

He was her soul mate.

She sobbed as she walked. Sobbed because she had planned to share the news with him that she was pregnant. Sobbed because she had decided to wait until he returned from his run.

She entered the now desperately lonely apartment that faced the river and framed the path that now reminded her of a black band to be worn for a funeral.

The plain gold ring on her finger was the exact duplicate of the one worn by Greg. They could have afforded much grander rings, but they had both embraced the concept that it was not the ring that would bind them. It was their love that would carry them throughout their journey together.

She walked to the kitchen and put on the coffee.

The detective that had called her had been discrete, but she knew, and she was going to deal with what faced her, but she would need a prop. Her hands would need to hold something and why not hot coffee?

Samantha smiled as she thought of the time, she had confided to Greg about her coffee cup trick to stay in control of a difficult meeting situation.

He had smiled and told her that they would only drink tea during their personal discussions.

God how she loved that man.

Alex looked at the report to make sure that she had an apartment number in the report she had on her desk. This she thought would not be an easy meeting. She needed to extract information that might be very personal. It would be like pouring salt on an open wound.

She and Trey drove down to the apartments and parked in the basement garage. The elevator to the fourth floor rose smoothly and silently. She looked at Trey and asked if he was ready for this interview.

He commented that in his experience there was no way to be ready to absorb the pain that permeated these types of interviews. He was not concerned about sitting with Samantha and listening to her anger, to see her tears, to feel her anguish. He was concerned about later when he replayed this in the middle of the night as a nightmare.

Alex made note that she would need to take some sort of action to reduce the stress that Trey seemed to personalize. Her similar experiences had once before taken her to the emotional bottom. It took time and hard work to fight her way back up.

She pushed the doorbell to apartment four hundred.

Samantha took a deep breath and slowly opened the door. She was surprised at the look of the person introducing herself as Alex Evercrest lead investigator and at the person that introduced himself as Trey McGregor.

The uncanny similarity of the detective to Greg's appearance startled her.

They stood with the door open looking at each other.

She realized they were waiting for her to invite them in.

She had arranged the room so she would have her back to the window that looked out over the river. She pointed to the couch and asked them to take a seat.

She then asked if they would like some coffee. She noted that Alex had immediately accepted, and that Trey had declined.

She asked if he would like some tea. He replied that if it were handy, he could use a tea.

Samantha did not believe messages from above but to her Trey's selection of tea had taken on the visage of a message from Greg.

The message was to help these detectives nail the killer.

Samantha went to the kitchen and returned a few minutes later with two coffee's and a tea.

Alex asked Samantha to describe the evening that Greg went missing.

Samantha decided to take charge versus having her soul exposed in a series of linear questions.

She explained that Greg has taken the day off to prepare a surprise birthday dinner. She described the dinner, the red candles, the expensive rose' wine and the formal table setting, in front of the window that was behind her.

She commented that Greg had really surprised her, and she loved the fact that he had greeted her at the door with a bouquet of a dozen mixed red and yellow roses.

She put her hand up while she got control of her emotions. She was having trouble talking and her eyes were tearing.

After a pause, she resumed and described eating, having a dance to the song that had been played for the first dance at the wedding.

She went on to explain that Greg had been preparing for the Flying Pig Marathon and had suggested saving desert for after he had finished his practice fifteen-mile run.

He got into his running outfit, gave me a kiss, and went out for his run.

Samantha once again had to stop as her emotions took over.

Then she explained that the reason they were living in apartment was that they were buying a home and they both worked in the twin towers. They had purchased a house in Price Hill, but it needed massive remodeling, and they were waiting for it to be finished.

Samantha explained that Greg had grown up in Cincinnati. He had recently been promoted and had returned to his business center from a plant assignment.

Alex was not taking any notes. She was glued to the narrative and was having to control her own emotions.

It became clear to her that Greg had been in the wrong place at the wrong time. Fate!

Samantha looked from Alex to Trey.

Then she began to cry. She saw that Trey had bowed his head and his hand were trembling.

She put up her hand as Alex was in the process of standing up. "Give me a moment," she said.

Alex nodded and sat down.

Samantha dried her tears, and quietly said, "I am so mad that I want to shoot and maim and torture the person that took my soul mate. I know that sounds like I have gone over the edge. But Greg had wanted to celebrate with desert on his return and I wanted to surprise him by letting him know that I was pregnant."

It was heart wrenching. It made Alex feel the opening of the black abyss that she had so carefully closed.

Alex looked over at Trey's shaking hands and knew that he had been taken to his edge as well.

He stood up and walked to the window and stood looking out.

Samantha confided that she had not yet told Greg's or her parents about her being pregnant. She planned to wait until she was confident that her pregnancy was going well.

Alex decided to ask for a refill of her coffee. She needed a moment to get the interview back in her control.

Samantha agreed that some more hot coffee would help. She had not even taken a sip of her coffee, but it was cold.

She came out with another two cups of coffee and one cup of tea. She gave Alex her cup, put her own cup on the coffee table and went to where Trey was still standing looking out the window.

She could tell that tears had run down his face. Samantha told him that she had spent every day since her birthday standing looking out the window crying. She confided that it seemed to help her. She suggested that he envision and focus on something that made him happy. Her vision was the birth and raising of Greg's and her child. That thought seemed to help her.

She asked if he had children. Trey said that he had a young son named Nolan.

Samantha suggested that he think about playing with Nolan and giving him a hug.

Alex knew that in Samantha, she had met a powerful, capable survivor.

She had only a couple of additional questions. She asked if Samantha knew the route that Greg would have run.

Samantha smiled and replied that she had jogged with Greg several times on the days he was trying to take it easy. Easy meant that she about died, and he barely broke a sweat. She described the path.

Alex thanked her and told Samantha that she would personally keep her informed about the case and would talk to her on a daily basis.

She asked if she could do anything to help.

Samantha asked about the procedure to identify and claiming the body and wondered if his parents should be present for the identification. She added that she wanted to have his wedding ring.

Alex suggested that it would be better for the parents to wait until the funeral preparations.

Alex told Samantha that she would call and let her know when to come in and identify Greg's body.

When they got on the elevator, Alex commented that she was mentally exhausted. She asked Trey how he felt. He confided that he felt like he had just returned from a gun battle where he had lost a buddy or maybe he felt even lower.

Alex suggested that they walk the path that Greg ran.

Trey commented that fifteen miles of walking would take them four or more hours.

Alex smiled and replied that it was only eleven and they would get back before the end of day and she would make sure he got home early.

By the time she they got to the car, Alex had decided that walking the path that Greg had run would take too much time and perhaps they could rent a cart.

She drove out of the apartment parking garage and went to where she knew carts were rented. She looked at Trey and told him the rental was on her or maybe the department budget, but he would have to drive.

She parked the car and walked over to rent what she thought of as a converted golf cart to be used around the river front park area. She let the attendant know that she was taking the cart along the river front path to the end.

She showed him her badge and explained to him that it was part of the murder investigation when he started to explain the cart was to be kept in the park.

Once on the way, Alex looked over at Trey. Trey had seen battle and had experienced the deaths of some of his platoon members, but this was Trey's first homicide in Cincinnati and Alex could tell it was hitting him hard. He had walked into an emotional maelstrom that he had not been prepared for.

She had not been totally prepared for the interview and could feel its impact. Identifying with the grief of the survivors and feeling their pain was how her trip down the black hole had started for her. It still had its impact, but she had learned to handle it. For her it would mean consuming another mindless romance book and multiple cups of coffee or sparkling water. Sparkling water, coffee, and tea were the substitute for the alcohol that she still fought to keep at bay.

She would have to keep an eye out for Trey.

On the trip out Alex was looking for and found numerous spots where an ambush or distraction that the killer could have utilized. It was clear to her that the spot for the murder had been carefully planned.

Perhaps the location had been picked because it was convenient and was located close enough that the murderer could kill and establish an alibi.

The ride was calming, and she could tell that Trey had come up from the emotional hole he had descended into. But as he had mentioned it was the nightmares at night that he struggled with.

Alex returned to her car more convinced than ever that she had already met with the killer. Now she would have to prove that connection.

She knew that getting hard evidence was going to be a challenge. She thought about it and decided that she would investigate Dianne's personal environment.

She would learn about Dianne's work environment from her boss and the one guard that she had sensed was not a Dianne aficionado.

She also decided to interview the neighbors that lived around Dianne's house.

She parked the car at the station and told Trey that she was calling it a day and that he should go home and play with Nolan.

She gave him a hug and told him to do he same with Lindsey and Nolan.

She unchained her bike and rode back to her apartment. She put on the coffee and picked out the book she knew she would consume along with the pot of coffee.

She planned to cry and drink herself to sleep. She had to get over the overwhelming sorrow she felt for Samantha.

The next morning, as usual she was at her desk, coffee in hand when Trey arrive. He looked better than he had all week.

Alex asked how he felt, and he said that he had spend the rest of the afternoon playing with Nolan and had read to him until he went to sleep.

He and Lindsey had talked things out and had gone to sleep early.

Alex liked his answer.

She asked Trey to look up names of the people that lived in Dianne's neighborhood.

She called Dianne's boss and asked if he would have time for a short discussion. She had kept the reason for the interview as low key as she could, but she knew that Dianne would soon find out.

She might even run into Dianne at the Taft Museum.

Alex planned to interview the neighbors immediately after talking to Dianne's boss. Her luck held and Dianne's boss had an opening at eight thirty.

Alex looked at her watch and was pleased to see that it was seven minutes to eight.

She walked over to Trey's desk and asked if he had the names of Dianne's neighbors.

When he responded that he had the info on the neighbors, Alex signaled that it was time for them to go. She led the way to the car, fastened her seatbelt, and drove to the Museum.

10 The Wife

11 The Museum Director

*A*lex took in the Museum director's office and knew that he and her both had the love of fishing as a common interest. She commented on the trophy pike mounted and hanging directly behind the desk and that at home her trophy hung over the family fireplace along with one caught by her father and another by her mother. She asked where he caught his.

He insisted that she call him Ted.

Ted then described an early morning trip out on Lake Michigan. Alex smiled and jokingly accused him of encroaching on her fishing ground.

Trey sat quietly watching the exchange. He was once again surprised at Alex's smooth and personable ability to connect.

Ted was curious why he was being interviewed. Then he was surprised when Alex shared that the pencils found at the river front crime belonged to Assistant Director Dianne Wrigley.

There was a moment of silence as he looked across his desk. He picked up a pen and worked it through his fingers.

Alex was impressed with his agile hand and wondered when he had picked that skill. She had a vision of sitting in one of the lecture halls and zoning out as she daydreamt about the wind blowing through her hair and a trout hitting her fishing line.

Ted stopped twirling the pencil through his fingers and began with stating that Dianne as a very good art curator. She had brought new life to the Museum with the periodic events she hosted. She had started an art-oriented contest where she asked the contestants to pay to participate. The Museum then gave the proceeds to various charities. The events also were very successful at getting donations for the Museum to run a variety of museum sponsored projects.

He explained that Dianne had been in several marathons and that her current injury that had her in a wheelchair had happened during the Chicago Marathon almost two years ago. He went on to explain that Dianne had broken her arm and her hip and sustained a serious concussion.

He had learned that the doctor explained that the hip injury was severe and had damaged the socket joint. Recovery would be slow and running in a marathon again would likely not be possible.

He also shared that Dianne was still very active in setting up events and hosting exhibits but that some of her early enthusiasm was missing. He hoped when she recovered, she would return to her old energetic self.

This new insight about her marathon experience made Alex even more certain that Dianne was the killer.

She thanked Ted and as she turned to leave, she asked the date of the Chicago Marathon.

The day took on a new sense of urgency as Alex thought about the tact she was taking with her current hunt for evidence.

She had no evidence.

The coroner was waiting for lab results.

The wife was grieving.

The Chief was under a lot of pressure to get the case solved. He had received a call from P&G's security director asking if he could be briefed on the progress being made and could P&G help in any way.

She decided to follow her instincts. She was certain that she had already talked to the killer. The pencils and her interview with Dianne and her gut all aligned.

The two matching pencils, one that had fallen over the wall and the other one that had been used by the killer.

The runner was in training to compete in the Flying Pig Marathon. To Alex this was too much of a coincidence.

The camera free path from the Museum to the river front.

Dianne's seeming calm during the interview had been given away to Alex by the movement of her hands. She was the murderer and somehow Alex needed to prove it.

Alex felt some relief when she found out that Dianne was a product of the nearby small town of Mount Vernon, in rural Ohio. This meant that it would make it easier access to her early history.

Alex remembered her training on profiling and decided that she needed to take that approach to solving the case.

She went to the Chief to ask for his support.

She described her ability to find a camera free path to the crime scene from the Taft museum to the river front. She shared the fact that she had traced the two pencils to the Museum Assistant Director of Art, Dianne.

But she was not able to get a solid reason or motive for the killing on the part of the Assistant Director. Except that perhaps she was mentally unstable.

Alex looked at the Chief and quietly said that there were too many convenient coincidences and that she was sure she had looked the killer in the face.

She shared her decision to investigate the environments of Dianne's youth, her high school years, and her college years at Ohio University. She was sure that she would either get new insight or would at least remove Dianne as a suspect.

The evidence was all circumstantial. She needed some professional help.

She told the Chief about taking a class on profiling and that she was asking for his support in contacting the Law School at Northwestern University. The professor she had in mind supplemented his income consulting for various police departments. She wanted his help.

She took in the Chief's look and wondered what his reaction was going to be.

The Chief looked over at Trey and asked what he thought about Alex's approach.

Trey replied, "There is no water in the well, might as well try to seed the clouds."

Alex had no clue about the meaning of Trey's reply, but it was clear to Alex that he was not going to say anything negative. She looked at Trey and he just gave her a wink.

The Chief nodded and stood up and went to the door and called to Bob and Trevor.

Once they were in, he closed the door, and told them he wanted their opinion of what Alex had in mind.

He then asked Alex to repeat her strategy to catching the River Front killer.

Alex shared her thoughts. Bill was nodding his head. Alex knew that the gesture was not one of acceptance but one of understanding. Trevor was playing poker face, but she knew he would most likely have a clear, but negative opinion.

When she was done with sharing her approach, the Chief asked Bill what he thought about it.

Bill thought for moment and replied that coupled with spending the time to find out about Dianne's younger years and getting a good profile of what the crime scene revealed would likely provide the information that would either lead to charging Dianne or dismissing her as a suspect.

The Chief looked at Trevor and asked his take.

Trevor looked around the room and said, "We don't have the skills to properly profile anyone and neither does the department. I'm not sure that remote profiling will give us what we want and by the way how much would something like that cost? And think about the time to get all the information on her younger years. I will be an old man before Alex and Trey get done and will probably be going to Trey son's graduation from college."

The Chief smiled and thanked Bill and Travis and commented that he agreed with both of their assessments but none of them would be around for Trey's son's graduation unless the river front murder was resolved in the next few days.

He stated that he was glad that they were all aligned to working together to expedite the investigation.

He looked at Bill and Travis and told them that he was putting them in charge of digging into and answering the questions of Dianne's formative years.

Alex took in the look of surprise on their faces and worked hard to control her urge to laugh.

She resisted hugging the Chief.

She enjoyed the look of surprise on Trey's face. She knew that he had thought asking the Chief would be a non-starter.

The Chief looked at Alex and told her that she needed to coordinate with Bill and that she had his support in working with a profiling expert.

He would fund a couple of trips to Chicago, but Alex and Trey would need to share with him how they were going to minimize expenses.

He went on to share that there was a lot of pressure, coming from City Hall, the Chief of Police, and the Security director at P&G, to get the case closed.

He looked at Alex and told her she was the lead and if they didn't get this case closed quickly, she would be the first in line to the gallows.

He then told everyone to get to work.

Alex suggested using the large meeting room to discuss the case and that they should order in Pizza. It would be her treat.

During lunch Trevor commented about how well she was managing the Chief. Alex smiled and replied that it was the only way she was able to get he and Bill do any work for her.

Bill's simple response of, "touche`!" signaled that she had interpreted Trevor's comments as a negative dig, correctly.

She went on to explain her decision to research the environment around her suspect. She needed to gain a deeper insight of why her conclusion that Diane was the murderer was right.

She wanted to know if there was mental instability in the family.

Was Dianne a problem child at school at a younger age?

What had her college experience shown of her character?

What had her time at the Museum been like?

She explained that each question mark needed some research.

She looked at Trevor and told him that she was sure he would think up additional good ideas as he investigated and that he should consider even the little thing, that might be out of place, as important.

They would need to dig deep to solve this murder.

Alex led the way to the coroner's lab. The lab was a place that not only smelled bad to Alex, but it also gave her the creeps. The wall made up of stainless-steel refrigerated body racks, the stainless-steel examination tables, the chill in the air, all made her uneasy and the bodies made her queasy. She could see, smell, taste, hear the silence of death and she felt the presence of ghosts.

She was always nervous when she was there. She noticed that it did not seem to bother Trey. She decided that she had to find out how he felt.

She was sure her behavior gave her emotional state away.

According to the coroner the pencil had been driven into Ted's ear and through his brain. It had then been rotated. It probably caused almost instantaneous death.

The coroner commented that he thought the killer knew how to create the kind of brain damage that had been inflicted. He felt that the killer would be someone with a medical background.

He commented that it took a great deal of skill to hit the ear canal with the pencil. The killer had a lot of skill or was very lucky to be so accurate.

He explained that he had no clue why the victim had been posed and arranged for show after his death.

The coroner's comments reinforced Alex's current viewpoint.

12 The Windy City

The thought of going to Chicago on an official police case investigation was a dichotomy of feelings. She looked forward to engaging her professor in the investigation and getting his guidance. He had been one of the professors she liked. Based on all the red lines on her case study submittals, she was not sure the feeling was mutual. She had earned an A in his class, but he always seemed to single her out to make suggestions on how she could improve.

Her visit with the organizers of the Chicago Marathon event was at the top of her list. After some difficulty and failure on her part, the police station operator had located the organization that had organized the marathon since its beginning.

Alex called the number the operator gave her and felt lucky when someone answered. She was put through to the marathon organizer.

He answered and asked that she call him Mike. He asked whether her mother had expected to call her son Alexander and when she turned up whether her mother settled on Alex.

Alex was just about to reply when he went on and said he thought it a great name and liked it.

After he understood her interest, he suggested they meet at his favorite Brazilian coffee house to discuss the case. He said he would bring everything he had associated with the accident on a thumb drive. He commented on the fact that the case had gone to court and the other injured runner was currently planning to sue.

Meeting with the professor and Mike were two aspects that were clear cut and would be easy for her to manage.

Her parents would be a bit harder to manage. This would be her first trip back in almost a year and they would expect to greet her and wine and dine her. They would also insist that she stay at home and use her own bedroom versus staying in a hotel. And knowing them they would insist on Trey staying in one of the spare bedrooms. She knew it would be hopeless to resist.

So, she decided that she wouldn't.

At the least it would meet the Chief's desire to hold down the expenses!

She then thought about Trey. She was not sure how he would take to a whirl wind trip filled with much more than just the case they were working on.

He would most certainly find out more about her personal life then she had ever shared with anyone at work. She thought about how to get him ready for a trip that would certainly change their relationship at work.

And she hoped the change would be positive.

It was the only way she could see how to handle the trip.

She would be upfront about what he should expect would happen. She would ask him to go along for the ride and enjoy watching her squirm as her parents treated her like a child.

The Chief knew about her mother and father, but he really did not know about the area and home where she had grown up. Nor did he know anything in real depth about her experience. She knew that she had been hired based on her degree but mostly on the recommendation from the Sheriff in Zion. As she thought about her previous boss, she put him on the list to go see on this trip.

She was beginning to feel like she might just manage the trip to Chicago in a somewhat professional manner.

She was walking her bike back to her apartment thinking it all through and wondering if she was on the right track. If she were right about Dianne being the killer, she had to come up with some motive for the killing that made sense. She thought again about the professor and hoped he was as good as the persona he had projected during his lectures. He would be the first on her to do list and the first would get done before she went home for dinner.

She suddenly realized she was on the fourth floor, standing at her apartment door. She shook her head as she unlocked her door and pushed her bike in and across to the bike rack.

She could not remember coming into the building and coming up the elevator.

After locking the door, she decided on one of the frozen pre-cooked dinners she had prepared on the weekend. She nuked a glass of mint tea in the microwave and then turned on the local news to see what the latest information they might be sharing about her case. She hoped that there was nothing.

After dinner and a quick shower, she hit the sack.

The next morning, she was sitting at her desk with her usual cup of coffee when Trey walked in. She made it a point to be one of the first to get in. This gave her the chance to make the coffee strong and to her liking and to quickly think through the plan for the day.

Trey waved as he turned into the closet sized space that served as the detective's coffee center. It was small but it did have a small refrigerator, a microwave, and a large thirty-cup coffee pot.

Once Trey had taken his seat and had a sip of coffee, Alex suggested they use a huddle room to plan their trip to Chicago.

Once in the huddle room she looked at Trey and told him that he was in for a surprise. The trip to Chicago was going to be very different than he might be thinking it was going to be. She explained that the business part of the trip was simple, as compared to what she was facing in dealing with her parents.

His reaction was to share that he understood how parents treated their adult children. On his return from Iraq, he stayed with his parents for a couple of weeks while he was looking for an apartment. He had been stressed by his combat experience, but his parents almost drove him over the edge.

Even after his marriage, when they went home for Christmas his mother's constant attention was too much.

Alex chuckled and said that he was going to experience a tsunami of parental support that would match and surpass any of his previous experience. He should expect to stay at her house, have dinner with her parents, and even go fishing if he desired to do so but if not, he would have his family as an excuse to return to Cincinnati on Friday evening. If he wanted to go fishing out on lake Michigan, he should plan to return to Cincinnati on Saturday in the late afternoon.

She on the other hand would stay until Sunday evening.

Trey replied that he would love to go fishing but he wanted to call Lindsey to see if it was OK for him to stay.

Alex replied that while he called Lindsey, she would call her mother and let her know that she was coming in on Thursday morning.

Her mother reacted exactly as Alex had expected. She insisted the Alex stay at home. And that her detective partner would get the big spare bedroom with the private bath. She would take the day off on Thursday and prepare a feast as a celebration of her "daughter" finally coming to visit.

Alex smiled and agreed that she and Trey would stay at the house. She said she looked forward to a surprise dinner out by the pool.

She saw Trey give a thumbs up to fishing on the lake.

Her mother was just getting into the reason she should stay at home when Alex interrupted and pointed out that she had agreed to staying at home.

Then she told her mother that she would like to go out fishing on Saturday morning, her mother said they should all go fishing. She said that it would be a great way to spend Saturday morning.

Alex told her mother she had to end her call so she could book a flight. She would take an taxi home but let her know that she would love to use her Jaguar while she was there.

Her mother replied that it was in great condition and that her father drove it to work at least once every other week, but she would make sure that he had it ready for her to use.

When Alex hung up, Trey looked at her and exclaimed, "You ride a bike into work every day, but you have a Jaguar at home sitting in the garage!" Your right I am already getting to know stuff about you that you have never shared. I am now wondering about the other things I will find out. I think I am really going to enjoy this official business trip.

I will only say, "Be gentle with your exposure, it's my first time."

Alex quietly told Trey that he had to promise to keep what he found out about her quiet. It was OK to share it with Lindsey, but he should be quiet at work.

She told him that the Jag was an old one with the twelve-cylinder engine. It was dark green with leather interior. Her father had given it to her when she was a high school senior.

The Jag was then fifteen years old. It was now twenty-five years old and for her it was a treasure to be enjoyed periodically and taken care of meticulously.

Trey nodded and replied that he would keep what he found out to enjoy by himself. He smiled and went on to say that he was really, really looking forward to the trip.

Alex asked Trey to make arrangements to fly to Chicago early the next morning.

She put in a call to her professor. She got his secretary, explained the reason for her visit, and arranged for a lunch meeting. She asked if the professor had a favorite restaurant near the University that she could treat him to. The secretary suggested a place and volunteered to make the reservation for noon. Alex made sure to let her know that there would be two meeting with the professor and thanked her. She got off the phone and listened as Trey finished making the flight reservations.

She was pleased that the flight left at ten and would land at ten in Chicago. This would give them time to catch a cab and make it to the restaurant.

She called the sheriff in Zion and arranged to meet him at his office. She made sure that he knew that she would treat him to a coffee at their favorite coffee shop.

She looked at Trey and suggested that they update the Chief, see how Bill and Travis were doing, and plan on an early lunch and then go home.

She pointed out that it would allow him to spend the time with Nolan and Lindsey so he wouldn't feel guilty about staying in Chicago and going fishing on Saturday.

The Chief laughed when she told him that she and Trey were staying at her parent's house to meet his expectations of keeping expenses low.

He thanked her and jokingly asked if Alex really had a choice about where she spent the night. He shared that he had once experienced the will of his mother when he had come home for a visit. He had no choice but to be nice while he was doted on by his loving mother.

Alex gave him a big smile and said it really was his insistence of keeping the budget under control that was driving her.

At lunch Alex asked Trey how the case was affecting him. He replied that Samantha's and her advice to focus on the good things in his life had helped. He said that he had come to Cincinnati because he was looking for a police department that didn't have to handle the crazy things going on in Minneapolis. It was not working out the way he had hoped.

Alex looked over at him and told him she had chosen Cincinnati because it had the crime and murder rate of cities like Chicago, New York, and LA. She had wanted the small-town feel, but the big city crime scene.

Trey bent his head and said he should have been more thorough in his job hunting but it was too late. He not only had to be investigating one of the weirdest crimes he could imagine but he also had to go spend the rest of the week with his partner's parents.

13 "Be a Hero"

Bruce watched as Alex walked out of his office and quietly closed the door. He was pleased with the initiative that Alex was taking. She was everything he had hope he was getting when he hired her. He wished there were more direct evidence for the case she was now on. He had initially looked into what Alex was doing. He wanted to be certain that she was not missing any critical part of the investigation. He couldn't see anything more she could do.

Her idea to use a crime scene profiler was a great idea. He had enrolled Bill and Travis so that the load could be split. The pressure on him to solve the case was increasing daily.

He desperately needed the case solved.

Through the window, he watched as Alex led the team into a huddle room. It was clear she was in charge. She was laughing as she talked to Bill and Travis. He wished he could be in the room to hear the exchange. It was clear to him that Alex and Travis exchanged a few barbs. Travis was a bit of a pain, but he was a good detective. Bill was solid as a rock.

He was sure the four, led by Alex would get the killer. He hoped they would close the case sooner than later.

He turned and walked back to the phone ringing in his office. The voice on the other end was his boss. He was asked if he was watching the news. He turned on his TV and watched as the press named the river front murder, the "Pencil Dick Murder" and were reporting that the police had no suspect and no leads in the case.

His boss wanted to know who on the force had given the press the information. Bruce replied that it had not come from the detectives and that he was talking to the boss of the rest of the police department and that he should go ask his people.

The "Don't get smart with me," from his boss reminded Bruce that the two of them were always one step away from a confrontation. He really needed to figure out how to get a new boss. This one was an ass and certainly, had no concern but what the news might say about him.

His boss indicated that he wanted the best people on the case, and he wanted it solved quickly.

Bruce assured his boss that the best detectives were on the case.

He usually left his office door open. He would have preferred a desk out on the floor. Now he was contemplating his staff. He had four detective pairs. He wondered if he needed more.

He decided that more was not in the cards, but he thought again about the question Alex asked about profiling. He had not thought about it before but now he saw that profiling skill training should be something they all would benefit from.

He reached for his phone and called Alex. He asked her to extend an invitation to her profiling professor to see if he would hold some training for the department.

He laughed when Alex asked what it would do to his budget.

He walked out to his car and took in the cars in the lot. Alex's car was the oldest one assigned to anyone. He had rescued it from going out to an auction house but had asked to keep that aspect quiet. He had been please by Alex's thanking him for assigning her a car that she could drive home if she wanted to. She had also let him know that her bike was her primary way of getting to and from work. He liked her attitude. She knew she had drawn the oldest car and didn't care a bit.

He got into his car. It was the second oldest car in the lot. He had passed up getting a new one. His boss had offered him a newer car, but he had turned it down. The way he had been given the offer of a new car had seemed too much like a bribe.

He had no desire to be "upholding" to his boss.

He drove home slowly. He was frustrated by the way the department was organized. He knew that somehow, he had to convince the next level up to get him out from under his current boss. The two units should be equal in the hierarchical structure.

When he got home, he enjoyed the hug and kiss that Mary-Anne gave him. During dinner he asked for her opinion on how he could change the police department organization.

The response surprised him. She told him that he needed to become visible to the community and to be seen as a city hero. She told him that anything less would not work. She commented that it would be impossible to just work hard and try to change things from the inside. The current structure was based on that approach, and it was designed to keep things as they were.

"Be a hero," was her closing remark.

It made sense to Bruce, but it brought out a laugh of despair.

"How exactly do I get to become famous and be a hero," he asked?

Mary-Anne looked at him and said that he had his super detective working the case. He needed to manage that situation so the news would put her and himself in the spotlight. Once in the spotlight, he had to speak like and act like the hero Cincinnati needed to have. She went on to say that the city council and the Mayor would welcome the ability to show that they were progressive and wanted to show the nation that they had an integrated police force.

Bruce laughed and said that it sounded like she was recommending playing the race card.

She looked at him and asked if he had any other cards to play.

14 The Competition

Bill sat at his desk and watched as, Alex, the new black female detective walked into the Chief's office. She seemed about the age of his youngest daughter. She was very good looking, and she was articulate. If things went her way she would soon rise to the top.

He thought back over his career and realized that he politically had started with a conservative attitude that focused on money matters and an embracing liberal attitude when it came to being fair with people. Over the years he slowly drifted from the centrist that he thought he was to what now seemed to put him more to the liberal side than the conservative one.

He had grown in experience and skill, but he was sure the world around him had moved as he stood with the same basic set of beliefs in the spot and position that he called being fair.

Or perhaps he was just getting old in a world that was changing so fast and on the other hand seemed to be stuck in a social quagmire where scared white people were reacting negatively out of fear.

He had always been for integration and giving everyone a chance. Anything else did not seem fair. He was not afraid of the world becoming more integrated. He actually hoped that the society around him could embrace what they were taught in church and in scouting. Just be a good scout and give a helping hand. One day men had to recognize that they had sisters that were their equal. People had to see that all persons wanted to have a good life and that a good life was possible for all.

He had wanted the position as Chief of Detectives and had been disappointed when instead, Chief Johnson was recruited. The fact the Chief was black had resulted in many of the people in the police department giving Bill the line that he, "should hold on" because the new chief would not last long.

Bill instead decided to be supportive and try to see that the Chief got a fair chance.

The Chief had recognized the fact that Bill had wanted the role as Chief and asked for his support. The recognition of his situation and the way the new Chief treated everyone in the organization instantly made Bill a supporter.

The Chief had come to him when he was about to hire the first female, black detective to get his opinion of doing so and to review her qualifications.

Her education credentials were impressive but would have fallen flat with him had it not been the series of jobs following her head of the class, graduation at Northwestern.

She had taken a job at a prestigious law firm clerking to a judge but had stayed for less than a year before she took a job as a deputy sheriff in a small town.

She took a significant pay cut to get closer to the street action.

In her introduction letter she had made the comment that being a lawyer was a great profession but finding and bringing in the criminal was more than great it was a noble profession.

She had commented that she viewed those protectors, in blue, or black or whatever the color of their uniform, as society's hero's. Heroes that made a difference for all of society and she wanted to be a heroine.

That one statement sent a shiver down his back. He was an immediate supporter.

She could have been green or purple color, and he would have supported her.

Bill looked over at Trey sitting at his desk. Trey was sitting there because when the Chief posted the opening to be Alex's partner, he had received no applications from within the department.

Bill had let the Chief know that he had inquired around about the fact that no one had applied and had found out that there would be no applications. No one was going to dare to be her partner. She had been, "Blacklisted."

He had discussed this with Trevor, his partner and proposed that one of them could partner with her and the other would partner with someone on the force.

Trevor had pointed out that then one of them would not have a partner and both would be on a hands-off list with the rest of the organization.

Bill had agreed with him and had suggested to the Chief that he should recruit outside of Cincinnati.

When the Chief brought Trey's resume for him to review, he was again impressed. Trey was a decorated Iraq war hero. He had an excellent letter of support from the Minneapolis Police department. He had recovered from PTSD. Bill knew that recovery was a word that did not really apply. He was sure that Trey controlled the situation that would be with him for a lifetime.

He found out that Trey had sought out a police department that might have less activity than the Minneapolis department.

Bill knew that Trey had not expected his first major case to be a weird and unusual murder.

He thought that Trey and Alex were a perfect match but was somewhat surprised that Alex was to be the lead detective.

Trevor had the opinion that the working relationship between the two would end in failure.

Bill was not sure, but it was clear to him in the short months that had passed that Alex was on her way up and Trey was becoming her staunch supporter. The two seemed to be in tune and were always smiling and joking as they talked with each other. Bill saw that they would have the same or maybe better relationship that he and Trevor shared.

Bill saw the Chief open his door and wave to him and Trevor.

He nudged Trevor and they walked over and into the Chief's office.

They listened as Alex shared the facts of the River Front murder. She was sure she had identified the killer and that she and Trey had interviewed her. The problem was the suspect was currently in a wheelchair recovering from a bad fall during a race she had participated in, and that she was in a professional prestigious job role. Also, the murderer had an excellent alibi.

Bill looked at Alex and asked what the problem might be.

Alex repeated her position that she knew who the killer was but had no evidence to charge her with. She wanted to investigate her killer's past to find out if there was some indication of social, criminal, or mental problems.

Bill asked Alex why she was so sure.

Alex lifted two pencils, each in their own evidence bags. The first was the weapon that had killed the person found dead in the park. The second was a pencil she had found on the river side of the retention wall at the scene of the crime.

Both pencils belonged to the killer, and she had admitted to recently "losing" them. Losing two pencils found at the crime scene was too convenient.

Bill agreed with Alex's position and feeling but voiced the concern about the amount of effort it would take to investigate a person's past few years.

He reacted positively about Alex's idea about doing a crime scene profile, but he pointed out that it was an additional effort on top of doing the past research. The fact that the department did not employ a crime scene profiler was an additional issue.

He pointed out that both would be time-consuming and potentially expensive. He asked again if she were sure.

Alex looked around and replied that she was betting her career on it.

He was surprised when the Chief asked him and Trevor for their evaluation of Alex's proposal of investigating the past history of the suspect and in doing a crime scene profile.

He thought for a moment and replied that other than the amount of effort required he thought it was the right next steps for the case.

Trevor's response was more negative but focused on the amount of effort required.

He almost fell over when the Chief thanked both of them for their opinions and told them they had just become partner investigators and that Alex would lead both teams until the case was solved.

The Chief assigned he and Trevor to do the background investigation and research while Alex and Trey would engage a crime scene professional that had been one of Alex's professors.

He listened as Alex thanked the Chief for his support.

She then looked at Trevor and at him and thanked them for being willing to help. She went on to say that she looked forward to their support and to the good work she knew they would do.

Bill could see the sincerity in her eyes. Her smile seemed to light the room. He was ready to get started. He waved her to the door and followed behind her.

Trevor followed him and it did not escape him that Trey was last. He had been in the army and knew Trey was covering her back. He smiled because even after all the years his old army habits and behaviors would sometimes surface just as it had just surface in Trey.

Trey had her back. It was a strong and clear message that he was demonstrating.

15 The Professor

*A*lex was pleased that the timing of the flight to Chicago had them arriving at ten local time. This would give them a chance to make their way to the Farmhouse restaurant. This had been the choice that was Professor Sieverts favorite. His support had said he liked it as much for their outdoor food service as well as their food. She laughed and said that there was a third reason, but she would let him share that reason.

Both she and Trey had packet light.

She had suggested that he use her fishing equipment so that he would not have to check any luggage.

She made the point that she and her father had accumulated at least a dozen poles each. It was a ritual for the two of them to spend at least an hour the night before a fishing trip deciding what pole, what lures, and bait they would take out. There was always one special thing each of them would plan for the trip.

The one common thing was that they always took out a variety of live bait. Both she and her father were constantly switching bait. If one seemed to work, they would both fight for their share of the bait that seemed to be working the best. Alex always tried to catch her limit.

She promised Trey that he would catch his limit, but he would have to fight for his share of the bait.

Trey laughed at her description of the bait competition but said he wasn't about to lose a fight over, fishing bait.

She said little on the flight. She was thinking through what to discuss with the professor. She also thought about her interview the next day with the marathon race organizer. She was becoming more certain that Dianne's actions were linked to her serious injuries in the Chicago Marathon.

Why the injury would lead to the murder of an innocent person was something beyond Alex's understanding. Perhaps Bill and Trevor's research would uncover some instability in Dianne's personality.

Alex must have drifted off because the next thing she knew Trey nudged her and let her know they were arriving at the gate.

She was surprised but ready to get out of the plane and get on to the restaurant.

The call from her mother welcoming her to Chicago did not surprise her. Her mother had no doubt checked on her flight. Her mother reminded her that dinner was at six and not to be late.

Alex replied that she and Trey would most likely be home by around four.

Trey commented that he had flown through the Chicago airport before but had never spent any time in the city itself.

Alex replied that this time would be no different. He was going to spend time on the Northwestern Campus, spend a little time in a café in the northern part of Chicago and then at her house and locations in Evanston. She smiled at him and told him he would have to wait until their next big case that brought them to Chicago.

Alex had called a taxi and was met outside in the passenger pick up area. The taxi driver verified her destination. She in turn verified his license plate number.

Trey had said he liked the lunch menu that the Farmhouse had posted and was looking forward it. Alex agreed to the good menu but reminded him that her mother was going to smother them in great food.

She planned to eat light.

The drive from the airport took about forty minutes. As they got closer to the restaurant, familiar buildings and streets brought out memories of her many bike rides in and around the university. She had eaten at the Farmhouse and the fact that she could not recall their menu only meant that they had been on her good but not necessarily great restaurant list. She remembered the great restaurant list because there were so few of them.

As the crow would fly, the restaurant was less than a mile from the campus but on foot it was at least a mile.

She was looking forward to reconnecting with Professor Sievert. She placed his courses high on her list of the worthwhile ones. She also hoped that this meeting would answer the question of why he had been so hard on her.

The area around and near the campus was a mix of hotels and residences. The Farmhouse was anything but a Farmhouse. It was an integral part of the Hilton hotel and was part of its structure. The red awnings over the outdoor tables immediately caught Alex's eye. She remembered sitting at a table near the row of flowers that separated the street corner area from the service area.

After paying the taxi driver and giving him a tip for his good service, Alex led the way to the restaurant. They were early and the outside tables were just being set up. She asked for the table that she had sat in last time. She chose the seat that gave her the view of the intersection.

They had just sat down when she got a call. It was her father. He suggested that after lunch she should come to the campus and show Trey around a bit and that when they were ready, he would drive them home. He let her know that he had thought about driving her Jag in but had decided against it and was instead driving his SUV that had enough room for the three of them and all their luggage.

Alex laughed and said it was so sensible of him to consider the need for more space and that she would fill the back of the SUV with her luggage.

She thanked him and said that his plan was perfect and that she would come to his office and then if he didn't have any more classes, they could make their way home.

He replied that his last class was at two and that he was at her service after that time.

Trey had ordered an iced tea and sipped it as he listened to one side of the father daughter conversation and banter. He could tell by Alex's look that she had a great relationship with her father. He already knew that she had a great one with her mother. He was a bit jealous. He had good parents, but it was clear that he was about to interact in a family that had extremely strong bonds.

It was becoming clear to him that Alex's self-confidence was hers, but it had as well been nurtured and developed by her parents.

Alex had been watching Trey and was about to ask him about his smug look when she saw the professor walking up the street toward the restaurant. He was approaching on foot coming up Church Street.

She stood up and waved to him. He responded by waving back.

The professor shook hands with them and sat down at the table. He waved his hand and called out the name of the waitress that was standing by the door leading into the restaurant. It was clear that he was a frequent customer.

She came over and asked if he wanted his usual. He smiled and looked at Alex and asked if this was on the Cincinnati Police Department budget.

Alex smiled and replied that she was sure that her answer was going to cost her and that yes it was.

He looked at the waitress and pointed to the top of the section that in all caps stated, "Honest to the Heartland." He pointed to the first item, Market Steak, and announced that it was time to celebrate with his favorite student and to make her pay for all the hard times she had given him.

Alex laughed at his announcement and replied that he was the one that had given her a tough time.

He replied that he had been easy on her. And he held up the folder he had with him and went on to say that she had not picked up her last assignment and she was going to have her read it before he would talk to her about her case.

Alex was surprised that he still had her report. She was more surprised when she opened the folder and saw scrawled across the page, *"my favorite and brightest student," "you EARNED an A" in my class, "Don't get stuck behind a desk, get out and take the world by the throat."*

She stood up and went around the table and gave him a hug. She had not anticipated such a gesture. She had tears in her eyes. She wished she had been brave enough to retrieve her paper when she had graduated.

The professor thanked her for having challenged him and that it seemed that she was indeed following his advice. He suggested that she should let her partner read not only what he had written on the paper but the paper itself.

He told Trey that the paper was to answer the question, *"Who are the hero's in the justice system and rank them in the order you believe that I should consider them."*

Alex handed the folder to Trey. She commented that this was one of the things he was learning about her that he could not share outside his family and if he laughed there would be no fishing on Saturday.

Trey laughed and pointed out that he had laughed before opening the folder. When he opened the folder, he was really surprised at the comments. He would have loved to have been in the same class as Alex and wondered how the other students felt about her.

The paper was another surprise. Alex had ranked that being a foot on the ground first responder lawman as number one on the list of heroes in the justice system.

The second position was to be a prosecutor.

The third position a defense lawyer and the fourth was to be a judge.

Alex had also written a section on the other first responder heroes. These she gave credit to the persons that rushed toward the problem and tried to mitigate disaster.

The paper really added a depth to how he now understood Alex.

He looked at her and said, "Wow," and gave her the folder back as he looked at her and gave her a nod. He told her that he was going to share this with Lindsey. It was impressive.

His Double Smashed Cheeseburger order arrived, and it was huge. It came with fries, pickles and some buns and butter. He took a moment, cut the burger in half, and pushed half over to Alex.

Alex thanked him for the "Wow" and for the half of the Cheeseburger that he pushed over to her.

She had not ordered. She had been so distracted by the paper and the memories it brought to her.

She was still trying to recover from the Professor's surprise.

The professor accepted his steak from the waitress and smiled. He said that he was anxious to hear about the case and he was also very excited to have been asked to give some profiling classes in Cincinnati.

Alex replied that her Chief was hoping to get an acceptance to having the profiling classes and saw it as an opportunity to improve the department. She asked how large the class could be.

The discussion during the meal focused on class size and how many classes. It was clear the professor was enjoying his steak. Not only were his many faces and sounds expressive but he also kept repeating how good the steak so generously bestowed on him by the Cincinnati police department tasted.

Once the table was cleared, and the coffee, tea and desert had been attended to, Alex opened her folder and took out her notes and pictures. She went slowly through the crime scene. Pointed out where she had found the second pencil. The first one was of course the one that was the murder weapon.

She went into the history and details of the victim and then into the details of her suspect. She had made sure that she did not divulge the person whom she suspected or the gender of her suspect.

Her presentation took her to the end of the professor's desert. He had been almost silent throughout the presentation. He had asked a few questions about the crime scene and had asked about the victim. He had not asked about the killer.

He put up his hand in a gesture indicating that he had enough.

He looked at her and commented that she had gone on for a good thirty minutes and had not touched her iced tea. He made the point that he was done for the day and would like to indulge in a Modelo Negra and motioned to the waitress.

He asked for a Modelo and for a new round of iced teas. He stood up and said that he was going of take a few moments and take a walk to settle his lunch and to think through what he had just heard.

Alex nodded her head and replied that he should take all the time that he needed. She excused herself and headed to the lady's room.

The lady's room was part of the hotel and was elegant in its décor. It had a large entry area with several comfortable chairs to sit in and beyond that was the sink and stall area. She was impressed!

The thought came to her that the Farmhouse would be as much remembered for its facilities as well as making a good burger. It had moved up to a restaurant that would be memorable for several reasons.

Alex returned to the table and Trey commented that he had been impressed by the visit he had taken to the restroom and asked about the lady's room. Alex replied that it was one of the best lady's room she had been in.

The professor came around the corner and sat down. The waitress seemed to have been waiting for this moment and came out with the beer and the round of iced teas.

Alex commented that the dark Modelo looked great, and she wished she could join him in having one.

The professor lifted his glass and clinked it against her and Trey's iced teas. He toasted, *"to us, the three sleuths and may we be successful in capturing the bad guy."*

He then began with the fact that the bad guy was a woman who hated runners. Pinning the penis to the abdomen of the person she killed was a sign that she also felt unrecognized for her feminine superiority.

She is most likely well to do and using the pencil as a murder weapon, points to her being an artist of some skill but again a skill that is not quite good enough to put her at the top.

Using a pencil to skillfully kill a person also points to her being methodical and that she has had to practiced, the kill move, for a long time. He was not sure how one acquired that skill. He wondered how it would be done.

Choosing the river front was probably based on proximity to either where she lives or where she works.

He went on to point out that this woman most likely worked in an art supply store, an art sales shop or even at an art museum.

Alex looked over at Trey and commented that he should not look so surprised.

She looked at the professor and commented that he had correctly identified the gender and that the person in question was currently in the role of an Art Curator. The pencils belonged to her. She also had camera free path to the crime scene.

The one problem was that she was currently in a wheelchair from a very bad injury that she had been involved in almost two years ago in the Chicago Marathon.

Professor Sievert looked up and commented that he remembered that accident. It had made the news because of the seriousness of the injuries. He commented that the organizers of the marathon would most likely have more details about what happened. He remembered that the case had gone in front of a judge but had been dismissed.

Alex let him know about the interview she had scheduled with the marathon organizers.

She was pleased when the professor asked if he could join her in the meeting. The next day was his grading day, and it was a day with no classes scheduled.

Alex was overjoyed. She felt that his participation would greatly enhance the interview and he would be able to give his evaluation and recommendation on how to proceed with the case.

She gave the professor the time and address of the Brazilian coffee shop where the meeting was to be held.

He replied that he would meet her there. He looked forward to a strong cup of the Brazilian black brew.

Alex paid for the lunch, and they began their walked back to the campus. The very next block had a series of restaurants that she had tried. She had tried the Vietnamese restaurant, the Irish Pub, breakfast at Freddies. She remembered the many rides along the street. She had come to this location frequently because she liked to study at the Evanston Public Library located only a block from these restaurants.

At the corner of Church and Hinman Avenue was the Episcopal church that Alex thought the street was named after. They took a left turn. This took them toward the campus.

The green leaves of the maple and the occasional oak that lined both sides of the street created a peaceful atmosphere. The houses along the street were a mix of brick or stone-sided structures and they all seemed to feature an inviting porch.

The transition onto the campus was almost organic. The admissions office seemed to be off campus. But its location near Clark Street was the transition onto the Northwestern campus.

During the walk Alex shared her brief work history with the professor. He nodded and commented that her inner guide had taken her to the job she would most like at this stage of her career.

He commented that she should think out some ten or fifteen years and envision the path that knowledge and experience would create and where she would want to be. He suggested that perhaps she should return to her alma mater as a professor in the field of law.

Hinman ended in front of a set of student dorms. The professor said that this was his point of departure. He had a short cut from here to his office that would take him between the dorms. He stated that he knew that her father's office was up toward the main campus.

Professor Sievert again shook hands and commented on how pleased he was to be working with them.

He made the point that this first session in profiling was on him especially if both the lunch and tomorrow's Brazilian coffee was on the department. He smiled and said he would get even with the many courses he would be teaching to the Cincinnati police department. He hinted that he had a great graduate student that was looking for a temporary position for the coming semester.

Alex smiled and told him that she would support his endeavors and would see if the Chief had a way to include a student in the budget.

He said that he was sure that she knew the way and that following Sheridan Road would take her to the campus center.

Alex thanked him and said that she would take his advice and think to her future.

She finished by thanking him for volunteering to participate in the following day's meeting with the Chicago Marathon organizers.

Then she turned and walked around the long bend made by the street.

Now she was thinking about giving Trey a brief walk-through tour on the way to her father's office.

16 The Family

She gave a last wave in the direction of the professor as she led the way to the library where she had spent most of her time.

There was a path across the street from Emerson Street that led to the two places where she had spent most of her time.

The path went through a park like setting were students often frequented. There were always those out to get into the sun and those who chose to sit in the cool of shade to read and study. The cooling breeze from Lake Michigan made the area a pleasant place to relax.

She pointed to the Deering Library and the University Library. She commented that she often went for a long bike ride before settling for her studies at the one of the libraries. She also often rode out to the Evanston Public Library if the two libraries had too many people.

She continued the tour and led the way north toward the Leonard B. Thompson athletic complex.

It was now a little after four. She placed a call to her father and suggested that he pick her up at the Ryan Field House.

She then led the way up Campus Drive around the huge sports complex to what she thought of as the back. There was a walk out to the lake front that she had often taken.

She asked whether Trey was up for a quick trip out the end of the walk, a quick look out to the lake and then a quick walk back.

When he replied that sure, he was up to it and asked if she would point out the fishing spot where he was going to catch all the fish.

Alex made a point of pointing her index finger toward the far distant horizon and asking if he could see the spot.

He laughed and said that he was sure he could see it because he could also see the fish.

Her father was parked waiting for them when they came back. He got out of his car and gave Alex a hug. He then gave Trey a handshake and what Alex referred to as a "man hug."

Her father commented that he had been looking forward to meeting Alex's work partner.

Alex commented on a thin streak of grey that was noticeable in her father's hair. He responded that it had suddenly appeared the other day after he had heard the details in the news about Cincinnati's river front murder.

Alex gave him a side hip bump and said it was time for them to get home.

The drive home followed Sheridan toward the north into a series of upscale homes on multiacre properties that had stone or wrought iron fences. Her house had neither, but it had a long tree covered lane that ended in a circular drive.

Trey was impressed by the neighborhood as they drove in. He had grown up in a middle-class neighborhood that was well cared for, but it clearly was not like the ones he had been riding through. He realized that Alex had grown up in a much richer environment and he was surprised that she was so practical and frugal.

He had not imagined that she was a product of what he now registered as a wealthy black family.

Alex had been watching Trey and sensed that he was a little surprised about the neighborhood.

Her parent's house was at the end of a long tree lined lane on several acres of land. The house at the end of the lane with its two angled wings made the house seem much larger than it was. It always caught visitors by surprise.

The lane ended in a circle around a large, raised rose garden that seemed to be embraced by the wings of the house.

The four-car garage was to the right at the end of the wing. The square center part of the house that seemed to connect the two-wings was graced by a huge black two paneled mahogany door with four large brass hinges on each side and two large brass door handles. It had a formal, and formidable appearance.

Alex was aware that her family lived in a top scale neighborhood. This was a point that she had not shared with Trey. She figured it was a discovery that was best left to their arrival at her house.

The front doors opened, and her mother hurried out. She gave Alex a big hug and made the comment that her wayward daughter had finally returned.

She turned to Trey and on her tip toes she pulled him into a hug. Alex had warned Trey about the hug and watched as he smiled and returned her hug and lifted her off her feet.

Her mother turned to Alex and commented that her partner knew how to hug and had passed his first test.

Alex looked at Trey and told him not to get cocky and that there would be many more tests that he would need to pass.

Alex's father pulled his car into the garage as Rose-Anne led the way back into the house.

Her mother guided them into the main entrance and stopped to explain that it had been the entrance that had sold her on the house.

She pointed to the circular stairs going up and around on both sides of the foyer and commented that it represented an embrace of the house's essence.

She pointed to the hall under the stairs that focused the eye into a large room with a huge fireplace. That, she said, represented the warmth that was to be felt by all who entered.

She pointed to the huge chandelier hanging in the center of the circular entrance area that was complemented by a round dark walnut cabinet with a large black vase, graced by a golden chariot and rider, that glistened in the light of the chandelier. She said it was a reminder that people should follow their dreams.

Her mother said that the entire entry scene was a display made to stop a person so they could slowly absorb the feeling of what the moon must have felt for the sunlight making it visible to the living and loving beings on Earth.

Alex had heard this story many times. Each time it got a little grander and more descriptive.

She silently seconded the "Wow" that Trey had voiced.

Alex's mother then led the way into the high ceiling, grand family room with its huge fireplace at the back and tall glass walls on both sides of the room. The family room was the center of the house. The glass walls terminated at the point that each wing of the house connected with the family room.

Her mother led the way out the to the right onto the patio. She had a table with snacks out by the pool. She asked what everyone wanted to drink and told them to sit and relax. She had some sandwich makings ready on a tray and would return shortly. She said that dinner itself was some thirty to forty minutes away.

Alex asked Trey what he wanted to drink, and he replied that he was ready to accept anything that was offered. Alex offered several wines and several choices of beer.

Her efforts at hosting were bypassed by her father who walked out with two Corona's with a wedge of lime stuck in the neck.

Alex smiled when her father commented that he had heard that Marine's never turned down a Corona.

She excused herself and went back thorough the family room to the front where the suitcases were sitting on the floor. She picked them up, climbed the staircase, and dropped the suitcases off in each room.

Her room was exactly as she had left it.

The guest bedroom had been spruced up and some new pictures had been hung up.

She went down the back stairs that ended up in the kitchen. There she stood for a minute and watched as her mother was taking the food that she had prepared out of their cook ware and putting them onto the serving dishes.

Her mother was a licensed chef and could well have opened her own restaurant but declared that it would be too much work. Her current job paid well and allowed her to work and live well.

Alex asked how she could be of help.

She became the food deliverer and placed each dish on the table exactly where she had been instructed to. She observed that Trey and her father were talking about fishing experiences and the size of fish each had caught.

She walked over with her glass of Pellegrino and made a smart remark that she wanted proof about the size of the fish they were bragging about.

Her mother came out with one last dish and called them to the table. She explained what each dish was and a quick description of how each dish complemented the other. The center piece was a leg of lamb that was poised at an angle on a cutting board and placed in front of Alex's father. That was to be the first item on each person's plate. The rest was a free for all, but each dish would travel in a counterclockwise direction.

Trey commented that the dinner setting was awesome and was everything thing that Alex had warned him about. He was sure to gain ten pounds in just one meal.

Alex smiled and said, "brownie points, not gold stars." Her mother caught the remark, looked at Trey, and said, "Gold Stars" and you get extra desert.

Alex listened as her mother went into the prosecutorial questioning mode. She learned more about Trey's experience in Iraq and his subsequent struggle with PTSD than Trey had ever shared. Her mother's skill at extracting information was in full display.

Alex relaxed and concentrated on the different flavors of the dishes on the table. One plate was enough for her, and she sat back and continued to listen as her mother learned about Trey, his parental family and Lindsey and his son Nolan.

It became clearer and clearer how important Lindsey and Nolan were to Trey's stability. She was aware that he was still fighting the PTSD and that it resulted in him drinking too much.

She knew the perils of getting hooked on alcohol and was a member of an AA group. At the right time she would invite him to join her at a meeting.

Dinner was great and the desert offering featured an open-faced apple pie, or key lime pie, a variety of ice cream or a little of each.

Alex chose to have apple pie with a scoop of vanilla ice cream. She listened as each person chose their mix. She stood up and helped to remove the food and used dishes from the table. Both Trey and her father joined in and soon the table was cleared. Alex took note that Trey and her father worked together to rinse and put all the dishes into the dishwasher.

Trey it seemed was earning gold stars faster than she could count them.

After desert and dinner both she and Trey said they had a busy morning to get ready for and an early bedtime would be great.

Her mother replied that she too was ready for a little rest and relaxation but planned to do some reading in the family room before retiring. She thanked everyone for helping with getting everything cleaned up after the dinner. She admitted that cleaning up was the part of hosting that she disliked the most.

Alex had risen to go upstairs when it struck her that she had not checked on her Jag. She looked at her father and asked if it was ready for use in the morning.

"I thought you would never ask," her father replied as he stood up and waved for her to follow him.

Trey asked if he could come to see this Jag that he had heard about.

Alex entered the garage and gave a little gasp. The Jag was polished, and it seemed to glimmer.

Trey commented that it looked brand new. Alex heard her father say that he had modernized it a bit. The dark green paint job was new, and he had put in a cruise control and a remote key lock system that included a trunk opener. The engine had been refurbished. The car was in fact up to date in the technology of the day.

Alex stood admiring the vehicle that she so enjoyed driving. She gave her father a hug.

Her mother let out a moan as if hurt.

"You know that he spent my vacation money improving your car," her mother said in a dejected tone.

Alex took the cue and gave her mother a hug and thanked her for having forfeited her vacation money. She finished by adding that of course it was for such a good cause.

Trey had walked around the Jag and commented that it was spectacular.

Alex smiled and said he got a gold star from her and finished that now it was now her bedtime.

17 The Brazilian Coffee Shop

*I*t took a moment for Alex to orient herself. She quickly realized she was in the bed that she had slept in for most of her life. She looked at the alarm and let out a small moan. It was five-thirty in the morning Evanston time. That made it her normal time to get up. This morning, she would not have minded getting the extra hour of sleep.

She rolled out of her bed and went to the bathroom and got ready for the day. She made her bed and got dressed. She took the back steps down so that she could be as silent as possible.

The precaution was in vain. Her mother was in the kitchen. The aroma of fresh coffee permeated the air. The coffee pot was full.

Her mother gave a good morning and asked if a cup of coffee was in order.

Alex nodded and quietly said, "black please."

A moment later Trey came in from the family room direction. He seemed to be in good spirits. He looked around the kitchen and headed for the coffee pot.

Alex acknowledged his good morning and sat down on one of the high chairs at the kitchen counter.

Trey commented that he was still recovering from that unbelievably delicious dinner he had enjoyed.

He took one of the high chairs and slowly took a sip of coffee.

"It looks like three of us are early risers," he commented.

"Yes, I am always up by this time. And anyone praising my dinner gets a shot at one of my breakfasts." Alex heard her mother say.

"Oh, I loved the dinner," Alex immediately piped up as she beamed a smile at her mother.

Ok what do you prefer two over easy with a slice of ham or pancakes smother in maple syrup.

Trey piped up that their meeting later in the morning would be in a coffee shop where he was sure there would be ample opportunity for the sweet side of the morning, so he was choosing the eggs.

Alex agreed but said that she preferred just the eggs and a piece of toast.

Her father walked in and gave his wife a kiss and asked if he could get in on any breakfast being offered. He announced that he had the day off and was planning to prepare all the fishing gear and get the boat ready to go out.

Alex's only request, of him, was that there would be ample suntan lotion available. She joked that those from Cincinnati spent so much time under cloud covered skies that they were susceptible to any long-term exposure to the sun.

After breakfast and another cup of coffee, Alex suggested they get an early start. She suggested they locate the coffee shop and then take a quick ride into the Chicago proper. She suggested taking a drive along the lakeside and then returning for the meeting.

She knew that Trey would enjoy and appreciate seeing the city center. She made sure he had a camera to take pictures.

Her mother let her know that dinner was going to be casual and most likely a poolside cookout with each person selecting and grilling their choice of a variety of vegetables and a selection of meat.

Trey commented that he was already hungry thinking about it, and he appreciated the warning so that lunch could be minimized.

Alex opened the garage door and then sat down in the Jag and adjusted the mirrors, seat height and put on her seat belt. There was no key. She pressed the start button, and the Jag came to life with a low purr. She lowered the top which retracted and entered into the back compartment. She slowly backed out of the garage and pointed the Jag down the lane. She planned to take her time and get use to driving her wonderful car. She had no plans to get on any of the highways.

It was a thirty-minute drive to the south side of the University. She estimated the coffee shop was another twenty minutes farther south.

Trey commented on how good the ride felt and that the seat seemed to mold to his body.

Alex smiled and commented that he didn't need to try for gold stars with her, but she too felt the pleasure of the seats. She wondered what her father had spent in total on upgrading the car. She was sure it was more than the original cost of the car.

When they drove past the coffee shop it was eight thirty. Trey commented that the valet sign indicated that morning valet service was two times the normal fee. Out loud he wondered why that would be.

Alex conjectured that it was a matter of staffing.

The drive along the lake front went smoothly. Traffic was light. This gave Alex the luxury of driving slowly and providing some commentary on the little history she had of the downtown.

She timed the trip down and then turned around so they would arrive fifteen minutes early for the meeting.

She pulled up in front of the Brazilian coffee house and left the car out front at the curb. She requested valet parking. He was both the host and the person who would park her car. She requested that he be extra careful and handed him fifteen dollars.

She asked if the table in the back corner was open and that she would seat herself.

Trey commented that she had handled the situation well and had been very generous.

Alex replied that she had little choice. She did not want a scratch on her new paint job.

She took the seat that let her face the entrance. A few moments later Professor Sievert entered. She gave him a wave. It would have been hard for him to miss them since there was only one older couple in the shop.

After greetings Alex waved at the waiter. He greeted them and brought over the menu.

Alex thanked him and then asked the waiter what he recommended. She was glad that she did so when he described several combinations that provided new customers a variety of sweets and several different coffees to try.

The three of them had just finished putting in their order when Alex spotted a person most likely to be the person, she was eager to interview.

She got up and walked out to where the greeter had returned and was talking to the person. As she approached, she knew that it indeed was the organizer, and that the organizer was a regular at the coffee house.

Alex introduced herself and verified that he was indeed the person she was to meet. He introduced himself as Mike Meland, known to his friend as M&M.

Alex led the way back to the table and made the introductions. Mike greeted them and asked to clarify their interest in the accident.

Alex explained that her interest was to understand how the injuries to Dianne had occurred and that the interest was linked to a murder investigation. Her interest was in what had been captured on tape and how the accident had occurred.

Mike held up a thumb drive and commented that the footage in question was on it.

Alex pulled out her laptop and put in the thumb drive. She handed the computer over to Mike and asked if he would be kind enough to drive.

Mike clicked and the video came on.

The three of them watched the footage that began a few minutes before the accident.

To Alex it was clear that there was team blocking occurring. She had faced similar situations during bike racing.

It was also clear that Dianne became frustrated. She suddenly cut too close in front of a runner next to her.

It knocked him down.

At the same time, the Dianne's left leg was held up and she went down at top speed and crashed into the curb.

Her hip hit he curb first. Then her shoulder and finally her head.

Her hip hitting the curb first probably saved her life because it took a major part of the impact. Then her shoulder hit and took the next part of the horrific impact.

Finally, her head hit the curb and that put her into a coma.

In slow motion it looked like the undulation of a whip crack.

Alex commented that it was hard to watch and painful to think about.

Mike commented that the male runner had suffered a broken arm and a twisted ankle. He backed the video up and this time they concentrated on his fall.

It too was very bad. It was an open wound broken bone.

Mike said that this runner's lawyer was filing a lawsuit against Dianne for the medical costs.

His lawyer was also filing compensation for pain and suffering. He was correctly citing her careless cut in front of him as the cause of his injuries.

This was a new piece of information that Alex had not been aware of.

She looked at Trey and Professor Sievert and asked if they had any comments or observations.

Trey commented that the video supported Alex's belief that Dianne was the murderer, and it provided a convoluted reason for the killing.

Mike shared the fact that Dianne had sued the Marathon committee because they would not divulge the name of the runner that she had cut in front of.

The judge had asked why she wanted the name and her answer had been the reason that she did not get the name. She verbally stated that he should be arrested and put in jail for having caused the injury.

She would not accept the fact that she was the one at fault.

Alex looked to the professor and asked for his opinion. She watched him shake his head.

"There is no doubt in my mind that Dianne is the murderer. She has somehow misplaced her anger and aimed it at any long-distance male runner. My fear is that she will kill again when she is sued by the person she blames for her injuries," He replied.

The professor looked at Mike and suggested that the runner getting ready to sue hold off until the case Alex was leading arrested Dianne.

Alex watched Mike shake his head and said that it was too late. He had learned just this morning that the papers were to be issued on Monday. He would try to get it stopped but did not hold out much hope in doing so.

Mike asked what they thought of his Brazilian Coffee shop. He smiled and said that he was one of two silent partners. The hardworking person was the Chef that ran the shop and the restaurant that was adjacent. Mike shared that he was a financial advisor but was now only working part-time.

He was a marathon runner but in no way a threat to any of the top runners currently competing.

He suggested they try lunch next door.

Alex thanked him and replied that her mother was a chef and was planning on having her and her partner to dinner. Since it was already noon and they still had not finished the coffee and sweets that they had ordered it was beyond her capacity eat more.

She asked Mike if he were willing to be a witness when her case came to court. Mike replied that the entire staff on the Marathon committee would be willing to be witnesses. That accident had given all, many sleepless nights.

Professor Sievert looked over at Mike and said that he would be interested in lunch if Mike were to join him.

He looked at Alex and told her that he too would be willing to be an expert witness in the case.

Alex said that indeed the professor would be providing his profile as testimony.

The professor stood up and said that he would send Alex a formal written crime scene profile report. It would be supplemented with his analysis of the video.

Alex thanked him and after a parting hug sat down and took a sip of her coffee. It was half coffee and half sugar. The puffs were sugar and egg. The other sweets were jam and some sort of biscuit dough. All of it would be classified as bad for your health.

She took another bite and enjoyed the contrasting flavor of the coffee.

She suggested they take a drive to the beach and go for a long walk and discuss what they should do next.

18 Lake Michigan

*T*rey agreed that a walk on the beach would be a good way to discuss the case. He took one last sip to finish his coffee and wrapped the final two cookies in a napkin and asked who was leaving the tip. Alex replied that she would leave it so that most of the expenses ended up on her expense report.

Alex signaled the waiter for the check.

After paying she followed Trey toward the door. The greeter let her know that her car was just outside the door and handed her the keys. He thanked her for a generous tip.

The drive to the beach was quiet. She was taking the most scenic route along the roads that ran near the lake. She pointed out the street that went to her house and pointed out the road leading to the harbor where her father kept the boat.

She decided to turn in to give Trey a quick preview of where they would come in the dark of Saturday morning.

Trey commented that even the harbor had the feel of an upper-class area.

Alex had never thought about growing up as an upper-class person. This had become obvious to her after her high school graduation and later after getting her degree, going to work but even now it was hard for her to accept.

She drove farther north and then to the small park where she and her parents had enjoyed many after fishing trip picnics.

She parked the car and led the way to the beach. It was not especially scenic but the lake to her was like the ocean for those living along either of the country's coasts. The fresh air always helped her clear her thoughts.

She was thinking about Dianne. She was sure that it was a case of a mental breakdown.

Trey had rolled up his pant legs and taken off his shoes and was walking along the edge of the water. Alex often did the same, but she had opted to just walk barefooted just above the wave line.

She looked at Trey and asked if he had any doubts about Dianne being the killer.

Trey looked at her and replied that everything pointed to Dianne as the murderer, but he was struggling with the fact that she was a professional art curator and that she had a top-level position at a very prestigious museum.

Why commit such a horrific crime?

And how could she do it from a wheelchair?

Alex asked him if Dianne happened to be a clerk at some art store would it be more believable to him.

Trey admitted that her position was a factor.

But what about the wheelchair?

Alex pointed out that the chair was part of the recovery process and perhaps Dianne was now able to get around without its use.

Trey replied that it would be important to have evidence that the wheelchair was no longer needed.

Alex listed the points that needed to get firmed up to be able to close the case. They had to verify that the wheelchair was no longer needed. They had to use the crime scene profile and Dianne's attempts to sue for damage as motive. But to make it all hold together they needed to prove that Dianne had a mental breakdown or was suffering some mental transference of guilt to long distance male runners.

She looked at Trey and asked that if he were the city prosecutor, would he press charges.

Trey looked at her and acknowledged that they were still trying to take their canoe up the creek without a paddle.

Alex nodded and replied that was exactly where the case sat. She pointed out how frustrating that was for her.

She said it was time to return to her decadent home and sit by the pool and enjoy a beer, roast a brat, and just veg out.

Trey agreed. He pulled out the cookies and suggested they sit on the large boulders and eat them so they would have enough energy to get back to the car.

She agreed. She shared that the frustration felt to her like an elephant sitting on her chest. She told Trey that she would not be able to relax until she closed the case.

She also shared how it affected her emotionally.

She did not share that she had raised her guard about her desire for a drink.

She had mentioned having a beer along with her brat as the two discussed the dinner, but she would make it a point to keep it to sparkling water.

She never again wanted to wake up nude in a strange bed with no recall of what had happened. She had been lucky that a friend had protected her from herself.

After nibbling on the cookie, she skipped the remaining part across the lake. She sent several flat stones skipping after the cookie.

Trey skipped a few stones of his own and told her he would have eaten the cookie she had skipped out over the water.

Alex laughed and said she would give him a bite of her brat.

They arrived at her home by three. Her father was sitting and reading in the family room. His favorite chair gave him the view of the pool that was straight ahead. The huge fireplace was to his left and the view to the right was the front door. Alex had come in through the door that entered the kitchen area.

She led the way into the family room and gave her father a hug and said that she was going upstairs to change into something appropriate for lounging around the pool.

While she was in her room, she placed a call to the Chief to let him know that both meetings had been successful.

She added that Professor Sievert was looking forward to giving crime scene investigation training and he had been very helpful in assessing the river front crime scene. He would be sending in an official report on Monday.

She made the point that she had successfully kept expenses down and so far, the cost was that of the airline tickets, one lunch and one coffee shop expenditure. So far less than three hundred dollars.

She shared the fact that the organizers of the Chicago Marathon had encountered Dianne when she tried to gain the name of the runner she blamed for her accident. She went on to state that the circumstantial evidence was piling up but that motive and other than the pencils it would be hard to convict Dianne.

The Chief shared that the case had been dubbed the Pencil Dick murder by the local news and that his boss was really upset about the situation. They needed a breakthrough in the case. Bill and Trevor were busy compiling the background information. He went on to say that he wanted something to put on the prosecutor's desk in the following week.

Alex said he would have the best information and report on the case that she could put together, but she was feeling that it would not be enough.

She wished the Chief a good weekend and brought the call to an end.

The house was situated so that the pool always had shade on the side closest to the kitchen. The far half was the sunbathing area. The kitchen had a long sliding glass window that had a counter on the outside. This was where the food was placed.

Alex looked into what she now recognized as a huge refrigerator and found the variety of food that her mother had already prepared for the poolside picnic.

She placed the deviled eggs, the potato salad, and the condiments out on the counter. Her mother had also sliced some pickles, tomatoes, and sweet onions. Alex located the hamburger and hot dog buns and had put the additional items on the counter when her mother entered from the garage.

Her mother thanked her for getting the poolside picnic started. She said she would be back shortly to get everything rolling.

Alex told her not to hurry and that she would continue to get everything ready.

The poolside family cook out was pleasant but initially somewhat subdued.

Her mother selected some music to pipe out to the pool area.

She then asked about the case and whether any headway had been made.

Alex replied that yes, but all the evidence remained circumstantial and that no smoking gun had surfaced.

Her mother suggested that a thorough internet search might surface some additional information. She suggested searching through the social sites. Often people vented on these sites and were ignorant that this exposed them.

Alex thanked her for the suggestion and looked over to Trey and commented that other than getting organized for the fishing outing in the morning, they could spend an hour or so in front of the big screen in the family room and do the internet search.

She shared her call with the Chief who was looking to close the case by the next Friday.

"Yea, that puts a little pressure on us. I am glad that we are doing the fishing trip," Trey replied.

Alex stood up and suggested they get the fishing gear organized. She only wanted one pole and knew which one. She looked at her mother and asked if she was going fishing.

Her mother smiled and replied that indeed she was going, and she wanted Alex to pick the pole she should use.

Alex followed her father out to the garage via the poolside door. The poles were all arranged on the large bench that was in front of her Jag.

All the gear was in top condition. It was clear to Alex that her father had cleaned and prepared everything.

Alex walked up to the table and selected a pole and handed it to her mother. She selected two more and handed them to Trey and told him that the black one would most likely be the lucky one, but the white pole was also very good.

She then picked up a green one and declared that being selfish and self-centered, she had saved the best one for herself.

She watched as Trey flicked each of the poles, she had handed him, and agreed with her that the black one felt like the lucky one.

Her father picked two maroon-colored poles. He proceeded to put the other poles on pegs mounted on the wall. He then displayed the selection of fishing lures that would be available. He said they would pick up the live bait early in the morning at the dock area. He let them know that he had ordered several dozen minnows, crayfish, and worms.

He said he had taken the boat out for a test run and that it was fueled and tied off at the dock.

Alex asked about suntan lotion and was assured that there was a bottle of spray on in the boat.

She looked at Trey and said that it was time for the internet search and led the way back out to the pool area.

After returning everything to the window counter and cleaning the table Alex led the way into the family room.

She pointed out the couch that faced the big screen and said she would be back with her computer and then she and Trey would do some internet surfing.

Alex was out of her element in doing online research on people or in using the social networks her mother had talked about.

It quickly became obvious that her mother was much more into surfing the web than she was. She relinquished the computer to her mother who quickly found Dianne on several social media circles.

Alex learned that there was a before the accident Dianne who displayed a confident superior attitude. It exposed a Dianne that Alex would not have liked but who was very self-confident. Then after the accident the tone seemed to change to an angry and perhaps vengeful Dianne who disparaged other runners and especially tore into the careless male runners that were causing others to get hurt. To Alex this seemed to be an online admission of guilt but unfortunately also only circumstantial.

She thanked her mother for the help and said that she was going to get to bed so she could get up in the ungodly time of four in the morning to go fishing.

Her mother seconded the idea and suggested they all do the same.

Morning came all too soon. She could smell the coffee as she went down the stairs.

Her mother had a thermal cup for each of them. They all took the coffee and walked out to the old SUV. Breakfast was in the cooler and would be enjoyed out on the lake.

Once at the marina, each of them carried several items to the boat. Her father went to the bait shop to pick up his bait order. She, Trey, and her mother organized the boat.

Alex suggested that she and her mother fish from the bow and Trey and her father fish out on each side in the back.

The breakfast cooler was put in the bow and the snack cooler was put in the back.

Alex checked to make sure there was water in the bait and catch chests.

She then sprayed suntan lotion on her legs, arms, back of her neck and rub some from her hand on her face.

She watched as her mother and Trey copied her in applying suntan lotion.

Her father returned carrying a five-gallon bucket full of minnows and small crab and a bag that contained worms and grubs. Her mother sprayed her father with suntan lotion and commented that the last time he had forgotten to use suntan lotion and complained about the sunburn for a week.

Alex rolled her beach towel and leaned back on the front bow-seat and closed her eyes. She put her hand up to indicate she did not want the breakfast sandwich her mother was offering. She was going to get a quick nap on the way to the fishing site.

The morning sun in her face warmed it but the cool lake air blowing across her face made is feel surreal. She non the less got a few winks in. When the boat engine went silent, she knew they were at the "spot" in the lake that she and her father called their fishing spot.

She then said she was ready for breakfast.

Her mother caught the first fish, and it was a keeper. Trey caught the next one and it was one of the larger catches. Her father caught a keeper as well. Then Alex decided that she would try her luck. She had waited so she could watch everyone else. She decided that she would try her luck with a large grub. Everyone else had used a minnow and she wanted to try something different.

She cast her line out toward the west where she envisioned the shoreline because it was beyond the horizon. She began to lazily reel the line back in when suddenly the pole was almost pulled from her hands. She knew immediately she had one that was bigger than everyone else. She slowly worked the fish in. It was putting up a great fight. She would pull it in and then it would run, and she let the line out and then pulled it back. Each cycle brought the fish closer to the boat. When she finally had it alongside of the boat, her father reached down with the gaff hook and pulled up the largest fish that had been caught that day.

He held it up and commented that every time he was getting close to matching the fishing ability of his daughter she would pull in another huge fish and surge back ahead in the father daughter competition on who caught the bigger fish.

Alex was satisfied with her one catch. She put her pole away and sat talking with her mother. By noon Trey had caught his limit. Alex offered her remaining limit to him, but he declined. He replied that he was satisfied and that the fishing had been all she had promised.

Her mother suggested that they return for lunch out by the pool. Alex seconded the suggestion.

On the way back to shore Alex offered to drive Trey to the airport.

Trey thanked her for the offer but said that it made more sense to call the taxi driver that they had previously used.

Alex thought for a moment and agreed that he had the better idea. She asked if he wanted to have any of his fish mounted and that it would be her treat. He pointed to his largest one and said that he would take her up on her offer.

He commented that it was the largest fish he had ever caught. He asked if she were going to mount her beast catch.

She laughed and said that it was not her biggest and that they would eat hers for lunch.

Her father and Trey carried the fish that her father would give to the bait shop owner and the fish Trey was going to get mounted. Alex knew that her father often gave the extra catch away. He and the shop owner had become good friends and the shop owner, as he had done this morning, would open early and have the fish bait ready for an early morning pickup.

She and her mother gutted and scaled the fish they were keeping. Alex steaked the fish she had caught to her mother's specification. She knew it would be spiced and broiled in the oven as soon as they got home.

Once home, everyone headed for the shower and changed into clothes that did not smell like fish.

Alex returned to the kitchen and was greeted by the smell of baking fish. She saw a well presented cucumber, tomato, and mixed greens salad. She asked what she could do and was told that she should set the table by the pool and get drinks for everyone.

Trey came out to the table dressed in his casual travel clothes. He thanked Alex for having taken him up on going fishing. At lunch he commented on the great fish lunch and complemented her mother on the sweet potato that he had smothered in butter and a drizzle of honey.

Alex smiled and knew that Trey knew how to work his mother as well as she. He was a good work partner, a keeper.

She had considered driving her Jag to Cincinnati but decided to fly home the next day as planned. She made arrangement with the taxi driver taking Trey to the airport to pick her up the next day at the same time to take her to the airport.

She gave Trey a goodbye hug and told him not to be late on Monday.

It seemed to her that the two were going to become a better work team.

19 The Crystal Lake

*T*he clanging of the church bells on the stand next to the bed brought Alex awake. She felt terrible.

She was sure she had fallen asleep. She looked at the bedside clock. I was a little before midnight.

She silenced the clanging by answering the phone. She was not prepared by the dispatcher's message that a body that matched the MO of the river front killing had been found up in Eden part on the southside of the Crystal Lake.

She asked who else had been called and learned that she was the first person called and was asked who else she wanted to call in. She gave Trey's number and asked that he meet her at the station. She then asked the dispatcher to call and let the Chief know and that she would update him when he arrived at the office in the morning.

She thought about calling Bill and Trevor but figured that they would not be needed and would be in a better position to help her if they were rested and fresh.

She was certain that she would be overwhelmed for the rest of the day.

She got up and after pressing the brew button on her trusty coffee maker she proceeded to get ready. She was in the office fifteen minutes later.

She was just starting to wonder when Trey would show up when he walked in. The coffee was ready and, after the each had filled their disposable cup, she led the way to their car.

She drove the short distance up to park and parked well away from the flashing lights of three police cars and the coroner's wagon.

As she got nearer the scene, she spotted the first news truck arriving. She asked who was in charge, and a sergeant she had worked with before replied that he was but now that she arrived, he was at her service. She asked him to tape off the scene at the edge of the sidewalk where they were standing. He pointed out that the current crime scene was marked off at the official radius. Alex pointed to the news truck and repeated her request that he put the yellow tape barrier from the edge of the woods to the far edge of the sidewalk coming down from the greenhouse.

He smiled and said that he would tape off the other side as well and keep everyone back away from the scene.

Alex thanked him and then walked toward the body. She immediately knew it was a repeat of the river front murder.

She turned to Trey and asked him to check to see if the Museum had hosted an event on Sunday evening.

She walked up to where the coroner was sitting on the lake's retaining wall.

He made the snide comment that she should solve this crime, so they didn't have to keep meeting in this manner.

She took a sip of her coffee and replied that she agreed with him.

She walked slowly around the body. It was a repeat in almost every manner but this time a knitting needle had been the weapon of choice.

She slowly walked around the body and looked to see if there were any other items that might be some sort of evidence. She spotted a glimmer as she knelt looking away from the lake with her head down near the cement. She asked Trey to give her a tweezer and to hold an evidence bag open for her. She carefully picked up what she recognized as a small diamond and dropped it in the bag.

With her head almost touching the walkway she scanned to see if there were any other small diamonds. There were none but as she was about to stop her scanning something about the grass on the edge of the walk caught her eye.

She crawled over to the edge of the walk and using her flashlight she scanned across the top of the neatly cut grass. She was rewarded by what looked like two thin tire tracks that might have been made by her racing bike or by a wheelchair.

She asked Trey to hold the flashlight so she could get a picture. Then she asked for their tape measure. She measured the distance between the two tire tracks. She was thinking that she would measure the distance between the wheels on Dianne's wheelchair.

She asked whether Trey had any luck finding out about events at the Museum. He replied that he had not but that he would do so as soon he got on his computer.

Alex felt she was done with the crime scene. She walked over to the coroner and asked him about what he thought and saw. He replied that except for the weapon it was a repeat of the murder at the riverfront. He commented that this might be evidence of the start of a serial killer.

Alex agreed and replied that they needed to take this murderer out of action before another innocent person was killed.

She let the coroner know that the body was all his and that she would stop by later to hear what his findings were, but she was on call if he found anything.

She called to Trey who had walked along the walk away from where they were parked. He returned and told her that he thought the runner had come around the lake in a clockwise direction. Alex asked why he thought that was the direction.

He replied that the runner had his watch or fit bit on his left arm. He pointed out that he dressed almost the same when he went out on a long run. If he were coming down the hill from the greenhouse he would have turned right and gone around the lake in the clockwise direction.

He had also noticed that the runner had blood running out of his left ear. The two together made very confident of the runner's direction.

Trey went on to describe the set up. If he had been running and a person in a wheelchair asked for his help to get the chair back on the sidewalk, he would have bent over and taken hold of both wheels of the chair to pull it back onto the walk. This was the perfect time to thrust the knitting needle into the runner's head.

Alex smiled and told Trey that his walk had been a worthwhile one. It seemed like the perfect scenario. She asked him to document his thoughts and observations and put it into the report.

As she walked back toward their car, she noticed that there was at least one news truck from each of the major channels. She also noticed one camera man armed with a huge telescopic camera halfway up the hill to toward the Art Museum.

She immediately knew that this camera man had a clear view of the murder scene. This she knew would be on the local morning news and would likely make the national news as well. She knew the pressure to solve this case had just skyrocketed. It was only three in the morning on what she knew was going to be a very long and tiring Monday morning!

Once back in the office she asked Trey to document his theory about the runner and to check to see if the Museum had hosted an event on Sunday evening.

She was going to transfer her pictures to her computer and print them. She would then organize the evidence and write her report.

She also called one of her local all-night coffee shops and ordered breakfast for both herself and Trey. She had a breakfast burrito in mind and Trey was for two grilled cheese sandwiches.

They both finished their reports and had just refreshed their coffee when breakfast arrived.

Trey commented that it was really great work to get done with a full day's work by five thirty in the morning.

He smiled and thanked Alex for one of the best business trips he had been on and that he had fallen in love with her mom and dad. He commented that the trip now seemed to be months ago.

Alex replied that she too thought it was a very good business trip and that she had enjoyed both the trip and the attention her parents gave to them both. She shared that the family part of the trip was much better than she had anticipated.

The Chief walked in as they were finishing their breakfast and came straight to Alex's desk.

He thanked her for keeping him in the loop and sharing the insights that the Chicago trip had surfaced.

He then asked what they had discovered at their most recent murder scene.

Alex held up the folder with both her and Trey's report. She said all the details were documented in detail. She also told him about the hill side news camera man and to expect the political hurricane that would soon hit his office.

He thanked her for the warning. He looked at the food and asked if it was breakfast. He said to put it in her expense report.

He suggested a meeting in his office once Bill and Travis had a chance to get their coffee and were ready to share what they had discovered.

It was not long after that Bill and Travis walked in. They were chatting as they stopped in the coffee area. Once at their desk Bill looked over and asked how the Chicago branch of the team had done.

Alex replied that she and Trey had some new insights and that the Chief wanted to see all of them in his office once the four of them were ready.

She also informed them of the new murder with the same MO.

20 The Take Down

*D*ianne awoke refreshed and full of energy. She enjoyed a robust breakfast of waffles, smothered in butter and maple syrup. The sun was shining in through the rear window. Her hip pain seemed to have toned down. She was sure it was going to be one of her better days.

She flipped through the news channels to see if she had made the news. She was thrilled that she had made three major news channels. She relished the fact that her pencil and knitting needle used to nail the victim's penis was the highlight of what was now being called the Pencil Dick murder and Grama's Knitting Needle revenge.

She liked the twist the news casters gave each case.

She grinned as she thought about the additional weapons she would use. Maybe she would do an amputation to add a twist to the scene.

She spent a few moments reliving the scene of the video she had made of the River Front, Pencil Dick murder. She had included scenes of the park the lights across on the Kentucky side of the river and had added some classical pieces from Schubert as background music. She rated it a top item to enjoy.

She planned to do the same with her Grama's Knitting Needle murder. She was sure she could make it into another very enjoyable video. She envisioned a full library of video's.

She decided that she needed to be selective in the weapon to use on her next victim. She had selected her next location as the Union Cemetery. It was nearby and she could continue to use her current Museum alibi scenario. Perhaps they would label her next murder the Graveside Side Special or if she used the right embalming tool it might get The Embalment Special as a descriptor. She would certainly spend some time on deciding on the weapon of choice.

She was also warmed by the fact the news reported that a break in the case was not within sight. Of course, it wasn't, she was sure that the black bitch that was leading the case was clueless.

It warmed her heart as she thought about her actions getting that detective fired.

She went in early to work to verify the timing for her next Museum event. She planned to spend the next few evenings singling out the runners and the consistency of their timing. She had already done some early reconnaissance but wanted to finalize who would be the next star in her video and she figured the look of the runner might guide her in the selection of the weapon she would choose.

The guard at the Museum entrance door commented that she looked well and hoped she would soon get out of her wheelchair.

Once in her office, Dianne turned on her computer and once again scanned the news channels. She had muted her computer but when CNN came on and was going to report on the second murder, she put in her ear plugs and listened to the report. The report confirmed the lack of any update from the police but said that a report was scheduled for ten in the morning.

Dianne immediately blocked ten out on her calendar. She planned to enjoy the no news update from the Cincinnati Police department. She was sure they were clueless.

After what seemed as if the whole day had passed the clock indicated it was two minutes to ten. Dianne locked the office door and returned to sit at her desk. She held her breath as the news camera finally zoomed in on the stand that had been set up outside of the police station.

Dianne could feel her heart race as Breaking News flashed across the screen.

Dianne relished that banner, "BREAKING NEWS" as it went blasting through her mind. She leaned back to let the surge flow over her.

The announcer then had the camera scan all the news reporters that were present in front of the police station.

Again, the sight of the number of reporters caused a surge of pleasure close to an orgasm. This made it all worthwhile.

Then the camera came back to the podium and focused on the person climbing up to the microphones.

Dianne had an instant feeling of hate and disgust. She was surprised to see the black bitch being allowed to be the speaker.

But she leaned in and listened intently.

Alex walked out to the podium. She had shared her plan to antagonize Dianne.

The Chief approved but suggested she do so in an indirect manner that only the killer would understand. She was sure that Dianne would be listening and most likely feeling smug. And just as sure as she was listening, Alex hoped to trigger a fear response. She had to knock Dianne from her self-centered pedestal and cause her to make some mistake.

Alex wanted the resolution to be an open and closed case that had no holes in it.

She had put in a request to search Dianne's home. The Chief had assured her that he would get it.

He and the Chief of Police were both on the stage with her to show support, but she had the mike.

Alex began the report by introducing herself. Then she turned and introduced the Chief of Police and praised the support and focus he and his department had provided. She then turned to her Chief and introduced him as the keystone that kept the detectives working in unison and solving the cases that came across his desk. She made the point that under his tenure one hundred per cent of those cases had resulted in convictions of the guilty.

She stopped for moment and let the silence stretch out.

Dianne was frozen to the scene and waiting desperately to hear what might be shared about her.

Alex looked up at the sky and pointed to the morning sun that was just clearing the downtown buildings.

She then made the statement, "that as sure as the sun would set that evening," she and all the power of the police department would resolve the case in the next coming hours. She continued and stated that perhaps the setting sun would be the time frame for this case to be closed and the murderer arrested.

Dianne let out her breath. The bitch had so far not given one piece of evidence that might link her to a crime scene. She was irate that such an empty boast was being made.

So far it was all talk and no facts.

Alex then switched gear and went into detail. She held up a pencil but made no mention directly of it but stated that the police had the murder weapon used on the first victim, and it had been traced to the current suspected killer.

Dianne looked at her locked office door as the anticipation of a knock went through her.

She watched as her accuser then held up her left hand that had a huge diamond ring that flashed in the sunlight. The flash of the diamond ring accompanied the statement that the police also had evidence in this second murder that allowed her to promise in the same way her suiter had promised when he had given her the diamond, that she had the evidence that would nail the current suspect and lead to a speedy arrest.

Dianne immediately knew that she had missed picking up one of the diamonds that had been ripped off by her victim.

Alex stopped and looked around and informed the media her Boss Chief Bruce Johnson would field a few questions and that the Chief of Police would close the session and announce the time for the next update.

Dianne's heart seemed to take a few extra beats as she remembered picking up the diamonds from the sidewalk. But still no knock on her door, so she figured that there was still not enough evidence for the police to arrest her. She decided she needed to get rid of all evidence that might link her to the crime scenes.

Alex thanked the press and stepped back, left the podium, and walked back into the building.

Trey was waiting and congratulated her on having done a great job with the news conference. He shared the fact that the Chief had given him the papers authorizing the search of Dianne's office and home.

Bill had followed Alex back into the building and told her what a great job she had done. He asked if he and Trevor could be of help.

Alex said that yes indeed she needed their help. She asked Bill to search Dianne's office and confiscate all files, the computer and the phone answering machine. However, they were to wait until they were sure Dianne had left the Museum. Alex asked Bill to call in a crew to help move everything to the police evidence area.

Bill assured her that she would have anything that caught his eye, as well as the records and computers.

Alex led the way to the car. She wanted to be parked in front of the Dianne's home and awaiting her arrival.

Alex drove up to College Hill into a quiet neighborhood of small well-kept Tudor revival, light brown brick sided homes with stone walls on each side of driveways that led down to basement garages. Large old maple trees lined both sides of the street. It was a well-kept, pleasant neighborhood.

On the way to College Hill, she told Trey that when Dianne arrived home, they would let her enter. Then Trey should cover the back of the house and she would enter via the front.

She was going to try to gain entry by ringing the doorbell and asking to come in to ask a few questions.

The goal was to confront Dianne and to see if she could extract a confession from her. A confession would validate all the circumstantial evidence.

Earlier Trey had watched as a female policewoman had helped put Alex's wiretap on. Alex was also given a pin on broach that was a small battery powered camera. It would transmit a video stream that would be recorded along with the audio.

He knew that a monitoring unit was set up a block away on a nearby street and that backup squad units were also only a block away.

He was still worried about his partner.

Alex was being cautiously aggressive. She wanted to nail Dianne, but she also wanted a clean arrest. It was her goal to usher Dianne out to a waiting police car.

Dianne's house was halfway back in a cul-de-sac street. Alex drove all the way in, went around the cul-de-sac circle, and parked shy of the straight part. A black Chevy van provided the cover she wanted. The nose of her car pointed almost directly at Dianne's house.

She intended to let Dianne enter and get situated and then knock on the front door and see if she could get in before Dianne could destroy any evidence. Alex was hoping to recover the jacket or sweater that had the diamonds attached to it.

About an hour later Alex watched as a grey sedan turned into the driveway and went down into the garage. She waited a few minutes after the garage door closed before getting out of her car.

Dianne sat listening to the end of the news conference. She was in a state of shock. She was wondering what her next step might be. Then it hit her that if the police had all the evidence that they needed, then they would be at her office door.

They were fishing. She was not about to take their bait. She was sure that the black bitch had nothing.

But Dianne had kept her favorite sweater and had planned to sew the diamonds back on. Now she decided that she would have to get rid of it. She also had the River Front painting with her slain victim sketched out. She had planned to finish the painting and to hang it in her living room. It would have made a great conversation piece.

Dianne decided that she would tell her boss that she was going to go home for lunch and would return a little later to finish the day.

She wheeled her chair out to her car and slowly drove home. She felt bad about having to get rid of one of her favorite sweater. She thought she had picked up all the diamonds that the runner had ripped loose but she must have missed one. Damn him, she figured he was already dead when his dying reflex had clenched his hand on her sweater. In getting his fingers loose, she had ripped the diamonds loose.

Diane listened to a recording of The Danish National Symphony play the music themes from the movie, The God Father.

She arrived at her house and drove carefully into the basement garage. She closed the garage door and went up the stairs to the main floor. As usual she left her wheelchair in the car.

Alex meanwhile was also listening to music while she waited but her choice had been the theme music from The Good, The Bad and the Ugly. She was the gunslinger that was about to face his enemy.

As soon as she saw a car going down into the basement, she turned the music off and simply said, "Its time. Everybody be awake. Trey, go around back but stay out of sight.

She got out and walked straight toward the front door.

Once there she checked that everyone was in place and let everyone know it was confrontation time.

She rang the doorbell. Her trembling fingers visually let her know how nervous she was.

Dianne opened the door. She covered her surprise and alarm with a broad smile.

She asked if Alex was alone.

Alex lied and said that she had just dropped by to ask Dianne a few questions.

Dianne opened the door and let Alex in. She pointed to the kitchen and said that she was just getting ready to fix lunch and asked if Alex would join her or at least have a coffee or tea.

Alex had no intentions of drinking anything, but she accepted the offer. It would let her get farther into the house.

Dianne turned to lead the way back into the kitchen and waved to Alex to follow. She acted as if she was about to have lunch with a friend.

Alex stepped into the living room and looked through the dining room into the kitchen at a breeze way at the back of the house.

There was no television. Two large ocean beach sea scape paintings dominated the living room. The dining room was accented by a glass vase holding fluffy light straw-colored grasses at the center of a dark walnut table.

On the way to the kitchen Alex saw the diamond studded sweater on the dining room table with a handful of diamonds next to it.

Her eyes traveled to the credenza that displayed several running awards but what caught her eye was a picture of Dianne holding up a fourth degree blackbelt. She herself had a third degree blackbelt. She was now on full alert. She knew that Dianne was legally a dangerous weapon and had skills that she could use to kill.

Alex knew she had found the killer. The adrenaline was pumping and having an amazing effect. She felt like she could fly.

As Alex followed, her adrenaline was slowing everything around her to a slow-motion movie.

Once in the kitchen, Alex held up the search warrant. She went on to say that she would be pleased to have lunch and hear Dianne's explanation of events that she would like to understand.

Dianne replied that she would be pleased to clarify the situation and assured Alex that there was some mistake and that could be easily corrected.

She was thinking that she would immediately correct the situation by killing the black bitch.

Alex was on full alert with her adrenaline pumping full blast.

Dianne offered her a cup of tea and as she held it out toward Alex, she swiftly executed a low round house sweep that knocked Alex off her feet.

Alex stayed on the floor but hit Diane with a kick to the midsection that sent her back toward the back breezeway area.

Dianne recovered and in turn tried a heel kick to the ribs, but Alex rolled way. She was trying to stand up but was hit on the side of her head by a downward punch. As the lights slowly dimmed and the world seemed to be pulling away, she heard the crash of the back, breezeway door.

Trey had been alerted when the sound of the fight came through the wire. He acted immediately and as he came through the door, he was hit by a round house kick that caught him on the side of the head and sent him flying. He was lucky that he landed on the couch located in the back breezeway. He was dazed and trying to get his bearings when Alex stood up and called out to Dianne that she was under arrest.

Dianne turned and resumed her attack on Alex. Alex used one of her favorite moves and slid past Diane on the floor. Then she immediately stood and executed a back kick that sent Dianne face first into the refrigerator. As Dianne turned to resume the fight Alex executed a front kick that caught Dianne under the jaw.

Trey wondered whose bones had broken as he heard the impact. Dianne fell like a rock and lay completely still.

Alex instructed the wiretap listeners to order in an ambulance and to request backup support.

She looked at Trey and asked him if he was alright. He nodded and told her to make sure Dianne was still out and that she was restrained.

Alex pulled out two plastic ties. One she used to tie Dianne's ankles together. The second she used to tie Dianne's wrists together. She crossed the wrists and put on the tie to securely hold each wrist to the other.

Dianne came slowly awake and when she went to curse the black bitch standing over her, she realized that her jaw had been broken. She moaned and closed her eyes. She would sue the city and police and make them pay for use of excess force.

Alex read Dianne her rights and then told her that she should relax until the ambulance arrived.

The wail of the ambulance came to a stop as the flashing lights stopped in front of the house. Alex walked to the front door, opened it, and displayed her badge.

She let the lead responder know about Dianne's broken jaw and that once they had her on the gurney, the restraints would be replace with hand cuffs.

Alex walked back to where Trey was still recovering. An ambulance member asked if they were alright. Alex said that both of them had received strong round house kicks to the head.

The responder broke out some cooling bags and had them hold it to their heads.

Alex placed a call to the Chief and explained the situation and requested that Bill and Travis take over the scene at Dianne's house.

She told him that this was his chance to announce that at high noon the killer as promised had been apprehended.

She informed him of the situation and that she and Trey were going to be transported to the hospital along with Dianne.

21 High Noon in Cincinnati

*A*lex was still in a heightened adrenalin state that could be heard in her voice and the rush in her speech. The first thing that the Chief heard was that she and Trey had nailed Dianne and that they had the sweater from the second killing and that on audio and video they had Dianne admitting to both killings. He listened as Alex added that she wanted assaulting her and Tray added to the list of offenses against Dianne.

He liked her suggestion of announcing a "High Noon in Cincinnati" apprehension to the news media.

When he hung up, he called his boss to let him know that he was scheduling a news announcement about the apprehension of the killer.

He sat for a moment and let the feeling of relief flow over him.

His trust in Alex had paid off. It had been her idea to expose Dianne to the fact that they knew she was the killer but to do it indirectly so that if Dianne were the murderer, she would feel the need to eliminate any evidence that she might have.

It had worked.

From the brief description of what had gone down it was clear that both Alex and Trey had run into a very aggressive and action-oriented person that did not need a wheel chair.

The fact that Alex had asked for Bill and Trevor to take over the crime scene at Dianne's house indicated that the arrest had been very physical, and both she and Trey had suffered serious injury. It must have happened so fast that neither had a chance to use their weapons.

He was glad that no weapons had been used.

He had suggested that they both take the next day off.

Alex replied that she wasn't going to do so until she had a chance to write the report that she wanted written.

He had the switch board contact the crew leader that had been monitoring the arrest. He got their call almost immediately. He listened as they described the sequence of events and that when things had gone south, they had immediately called in backup and an ambulance. They had immediately driven their unit to the house to make sure that Alex had help if needed. All the backup squads had arrived at the same time. He had been first on the scene and had found Alex in total control.

Every resource played their part.

The chief decided to view the visual and listen to the audio before organizing the content of the "High Noon" announcement.

He called Rose-Anne and told her of the successful capture of the River Front and Crystal Lake killer.

He gave her a brief highlight at how brave Alex had been and what a great backup Trey had proved to be.

Rose-Anne reminded him that this was his moment and he needed to accept the spotlight and to become the hero that the Cincinnati politicians were looking for.

He gave a small laugh when Rose-Anne suggested they should host a celebration dinner.

He replied that he had been worried she would not suggest it and gave the list of those to invite. He said he would also set up an official dinner celebration at everyone's favorite Steak House or perhaps the River Front restaurant. He knew that he would be able to select from many of the best downtown restaurants.

It was almost two in the afternoon when he walked out to the podium accompanied by his boss. He introduced his boss and then announce that at High Noon, the police had apprehended the killer responsible for the deaths of two innocent victims.

He played the audio of Dianne saying that she had saved the two runners from embarrassing themselves by being such poor runners and that she could run faster than either of them.

He fielded a host of question and each time he took the time to put the spotlight on the fact that the Cincinnati police department had the best overall force and for sure the best detective unit in the country.

The question-and-answer session lasted almost an hour and all the while he had made every detective, or street cop heroes.

He left the stand with his boss and was told that he had run a great press conference.

He spent most of the afternoon taking congratulation calls. He got a call from the Mayor and every council member and most of the county representatives and he even got a call from the Ohio state governor.

The call he enjoyed the most was from Rose-Anne calling to say he had always been her hero and the press conference must certainly have made him one for the community.

Alex and Trey had watched from the emergency room they had been taken to.

They received a cat scan to check on their concussions. Both were diagnosed with significant concussions and told they should refrain from any strenuous activity for at least ten days.

Alex jokingly asked it that included serious thinking or other brain activities.

Alex enjoyed Trey's flush of embarrassment when the ER doctor, a woman, responded that sexual activity was off limits but thinking about it was "OK."

On a more serious note, she said that driving for the next week was also out of the question.

Alex verified that riding a bike was also off limits.

The Chief had received a call from the ER doctor and decided to drive what he was now thinking of as his two rising stars home himself.

He walked out of his office and let both Bill and Travis know that Alex and Trey were Ok but had been diagnosed with serious concussions. He took up Bill's offer that he and Travis could bring Alex down the hill to her apartment, and he could take Trey home.

Bruce knew that Trey live out his way and that Bill wanted to see them both before the day was over.

Once at the hospital, he waited for Bill and Trevor and they all walked into the ER together and inquired about Trey and Alex. They were led to a joint ER room where both were sitting in reclining chairs with their feet raised.

Alex was surprised but pleased to see the three. She made a point of thanking Bill and Trevor for closing the crime scene.

She then jokingly told them that both she and Trey had to sit down after listening to the stories that the Chief had woven about Cincinnati, the police department and the so, so effective, and brave members of the detective squad.

She looked at Bill and asked if his raise had come through.

The Chief laughed and said that she was right it had all been a huge fabrication and that they still had to write the report to close the case. And that they would have many days working with legal to put Dianne away.

He chuckled as he shared that Dianne's lawyer was suing the department for using excessive use of force in the arrest of his client.

He stated that the world was still right-side up and no there were no immediate raises in anyone's salary.

Trey laughed as he held his hand on the left side of his head. He suggested that the department counter sue for excessive use of force by a lunatic killer.

Maybe then the department would have enough funds for the raises.

Bill agreed and said that he and Trevor were on notice that a new and powerful detective team was on the floor trying to take the title of number one from them. He went on to say that good competition would make both teams better.

Bruce liked the new relationship that the case had nurtured between Alex and Trey, Bill, and Trevor.

He again looked at Alex and recognized her ability to enroll those around her and bring them into a more harmonious situation.

They all left the hospital together.

He and Trey got in his car and on the drive, Bruce asked about how he felt about the team dynamics between he and Alex.

He was surprised with Trey's reply that he loved Alex. She was pulling him out of the worst emotional slump that he had ever experienced.

Trey then went on to clarify that he and Alex worked out and sparred three times a week in the department gym. He said that she would always exhaust him.

During the arrest, she had used survival fighting techniques that the Marines had taught him as well as her own Tae Kwon Do skills.

He was learning the Tae Kwon Do moves that Alex was a three-stripe black belt master in.

He commented that he was sure that the conditioning and practice had saved them both.

Trey made the point that the kitchen sink and counter had made it impossible for Alex to do her normal snap to a standing position and had given Dianne the opportunity to land her punch and kick.

Alex's use of the Marine teaching, to roll away from the attacker when on the ground, saved her. And that his clumsy entrance that earned him a flying journey across the room gave Alex enough time to recover and then fully engage Dianne and to take her out.

Trey went on to say that the sound of Dianne's jaw shattering hand been music to his ears.

Trey commented that Bill might think he led the number one team, but he could not see the number two team because he was looking behind him and his competition was in front.

Bruce smiled, Rose-Anne had predicted that Alex and Trey were a perfect team, and they would soon be leading the department.

It was their first major case, and they were proving her statement to be true.

He also recognized that this team would be one that he would assign to the cases he thought would be tough.

He dropped Trey off then drove home.

When he entered his house, Rose-Anne was there to greet him with a kiss and a glass of wine.

Bill and Trevor updated Alex on what they had retrieved from both Dianne's house and her office.

Trevor listed the evidence from the office and Dianne's computer. And Bill did the same for what they found in the house.

It turned out that Dianne had a painting of the events at the River Front and that the sweater with the diamonds was also now in evidence.

He congratulated Alex on having flushed Dianne out.

Alex thanked Bill and Travis for being there when she needed them. Once they arrived at her apartment building, she was about to get out of the car when Travis told her to hold on and that both he and Bill were going to escort her to her apartment door.

Alex thanked him and insisted she could handle the journey to her apartment. She laughed and said that next time she would invite them both for a glass of wine or a beer.

Her head still ached but the feeling of having solved her first big case carried her for the rest of the day and evening.

She would have loved to indulge in the wine that she had alluded to when thanking Trevor, but she didn't keep any alcoholic beverage in her apartment.

That night, she had her first really deep sleep that had escaped her during the investigation.

22 The Wife and Fiancé

*I*n the morning Alex remembered both Samantha, the wife of the first victim and Gwen the fiancé of the second runner.

She called Gwen and let her know that the murderer was in custody. Gwen thanked Alex for having caught the killer.

They chatted for a while and then said that they would have lunch together sometime during the trial.

Her call to Samantha ended with an invitation to a simple dinner at Samantha's apartment and that the invitation included her partner and his family. They agreed to a Friday night dinner.

Alex then decided on a walk along the River Front. She needed fresh air. She would have loved some company to share her thoughts and feelings.

She decided on a picnic on the lawn where the killing had taken place.

Her view of the Kentucky side of the river was clear. It was near noon on a Tuesday and there were a few folks sitting on the swings, a few were walking along the river walk but she was the only person having a picnic lunch.

Her Pellegrino was her major indulgence that accompanied a sliced brie, lettuce, tomato, and onion on toasted sour dough bread sandwich. The mayo really brought out the flavor.

She lay back on her blanket and considered her future. She was thinking about Professor Sievert's advice to envision her future and then follow the path to her vision.

Her phone rang and she was please that Rose-Anne was inviting her to a dinner on Saturday evening.

She was asked how she was feeling. She shared that she was enjoying having lunch in the park and that she was feeling great. She then jokingly suggested that this was a secret between them, and the Chief didn't need to know.

Alex then called Trey to see how he was doing. The phone was answered by Lindsey. She said that Trey was in the backyard playing with Nolan.

Lindsey thanked Alex for being such a great partner to Trey. His whole outlook had improved since he had come to Cincinnati. Lindsey shared that she was a little jealous of Alex and her ability to instill such confidence in Trey. She was so happy that Trey was very much like he had been when they had first met.

She confided that on occasion he still drank too much.

Alex let her know that she was a member of AA and understood the effects of the work pressure. She asked if it was OK to invite Trey sometime in the near future to one of the meetings.

Lindsey replied that it would be great if Trey got into such a program.

Lindsey then put Trey on the phone.

Trey, Nolan, and Lindsey arrived at Samantha's apartment shortly after Alex.

Samantha asked what everyone wanted to drink. Alex volunteered to help.

Dinner was spaghetti Alfredo. It was clear that Nolan was enjoying it immensely as he sucked each spaghetti into his mouth.

Samantha commented that it was great to have them over. It kept her from moping and feeling depressed. It helped greatly that they had caught and jailed the killer. She went on to admit that it did little to reduce the pain and loneliness she felt.

She shared the fact that she had found out that she was pregnant with a boy. She planned to name him after his father. Having him would be a great way to continue her love for his father. The grandparents, on Greg's side, lived in Cincinnati and were being very good at keeping her involved. She added that it helped to keep busy.

The dinner went over very well, and Nolan enriched the evening by letting everyone know that Samantha was a great cook, and that mom should learn how to cook the spaghetti like her.

Alex thanked Samantha for having them over. She suggested they have lunch, the following week at a place of Samantha's choice.

After thanking Samantha for the dinner, the four of them walked out toward the river and along the walk to where the murder had taken place. There was a play area where Nolan would have a great time.

They went there and then watched as Trey and Nolan played the variety of games that were normally board games but at the park, they were full sized.

Alex suggested ending the day with a ride along the river in one of the golf carts.

The late evening sun cast long shadows and by the time they returned it was time to call it a day.

Alex saw them off and returned to her apartment where she read one of the many books she consumed.

Little did she know that she would almost immediately be drawn into yet another dual between the law she was sworn to uphold and those who chose to bend and break it.

The End

Thank you for reading my story.

Read on for a preview of **The Girl on the Grill**.

Imagine the grill of an semi-truck.

Preview: The Girl on the Grill

1 At the end of the day

Henry looked out his window and once again watched as his personal aid charged with finding new business, Mandy, left early. He had hired her at the request of Percival, a college friend.

Percival was trying to get his daughter into some sort of professional career. She had graduated college and then had gone to L.A to worked as a waitress while she searched for a role as an actress. This was a disappointment for Percival and his wife.

Henry was not sure he was helping. She was smart enough, but she had no ambition. She was involved with some guy named Ralph.

Not far away across the highway, Ralph was feeling the heat from the narcs. They had pulled in several of his people and grilled them. He was worried that one of them might be turned.

He was pretty sure his lieutenants and enforcers were loyal. They had all been through this before. He made sure each of them was well rewarded and he made sure none of them used the product they distributed. He ran a tight ship.

His current concern was his new squeeze.

He had met her at a party thrown by a long-ago customer. This customer had graduated from an Ivy League university and had become wealthy. He was still an occasional user. He was now in the upper circles of the Cincinnati community.

Recently, Ralph had accidently run into this customer and gotten invited to a party. At the party, he was introduced as an independent movie maker to Mandy, the daughter. For the rest of that night, she was constantly with him. He tried to keep his distance. She had pursued him. She had asked for his number and hinted that she wanted to read for him.

She had been with him every evening since that party. She normally left and went home but she had been around when many of his business meetings occurred.

He knew she was putty.

If she were pulled in by the Narcs, they would break her. She was book smart and had probably figured out the business he was really in.

She was a user.

She probably knew too much.

He had discussed this with his enforcer, Bradley. Bradley was one of the most loyal people on the team he kept around him. He let Bradley know that it was time to eliminate Mandy and that it had to be made to look like an accident. There had to be no connection back to them.

A few days later, Mandy was present when an important business visitor arrived unannounced. When Mandy excused herself to go to the lady's room, he signaled Bradley that it was time to eliminated her.

He saw Bradley give him the thumbs up and figured Bradley would take her for a ride and dump her body in some remote location. This had been the pattern on similar occasions.

He turned his attention to the business at hand. He was not pleased that he had not received notice that the person who was sitting across the table was coming.

He voiced his displeasure.

The response was that there was a rush shipment coming through that needed rapid redistribution. The order to make immediate contact came from Mexico. He would have preferred to have made arrangements to meet but he had no choice. He felt at risk coming unannounced.

Ralph nodded. He knew that any call would likely have been monitored. He was still unhappy.

The timing for a rapid redistribution would put pressure on him to do so without getting caught.

He offered the business contact a drink but received a no thank-you as he got up and left.

Ralph rose and walked to the bar and ordered a root beer.

He was ready to call it a night.

Ralph, in his self-centered world, with his feeling of control had no idea that his world was about to be turned upside down and that in the end he would be running for his life just as Mandy had run for hers.

2 Ambition

Mandy grudgingly accepted her dad's offer to pay for her ticket home. Her parents had been paying for her rent in L.A. She had just finished an angry conversation with her mother. Her mother had told her that the rent support was ending. Now her father was trying to mend fences. He was the family fence mender. She and her mother were always at odds.

She thought back to the good times she had with her mother. They had paddle boarded together at the Lovely Valley lake almost every good weather weekend. She and her father had also fished at the same lake. Those were the times she wished she could repeat.

When she entered high school, things changed. She wanted to hang out with friends and have sleep overs with her friends.

She started fighting over the way her mother wanted to know about her friends, where she was going and what she was doing. She didn't need a policewoman on her at all times.

She also stopped fishing with her father. She realized it was boring.

She was happy to escape to college. Many of her friends went to the top Ivy League schools either on their top grades but often because their parents were alumni and big doners.

She was happy to get into Ohio State. She had good enough grades and had just made the cut.

Her first year was one grand party. She rarely attended classes and only did so when it was clear she was going to fail if she didn't. Most of the time was spent with her newly made friends.

She managed to get her grades up to a respectable level. But she had no idea what she wanted to do. She had tried to be a member of the cheer leading squad but had failed at the tough gymnastics required to be on the squad. She had grown significantly from the petite young girl in college to a well-endowed but much bigger young woman. The young women on the squad were good looking, petite and small.

Her next thought was to become a singer. She had joined several groups, but it became clear that she was not a lead singer.

When she graduated, she interviewed well but just could not see herself going to work for any of the companies and salaries that had been offered.

She figured she would go to L.A. and get into acting.

That decision generated a huge fight with her mother. The fight centered on the fact that she had no money of her own and her mother was against the idea of her becoming an actress.

Her father was the one that proposed a one-year trial and that after that she would again seek employment and take a regular job.

It was now a year later. She had only gotten a few second reads and never landed any roles.

She knew it was time to go home.

She thanked her father for the first-class ticket. She at least would be sitting up front versus in the cattle car area.

It was a direct flight. She watched as the plane flew out over the Pacific and then turned toward the north. Out the window she could see the landmark HOLLYWOOD sign on the mountain side. She had tears in her eyes. This had been her last hope to quickly become rich and escape the drudgery of working all day for the rest of her lifetime.

Maybe she could be like her mother and marry someone who made enough money that she could invest. Her mother earned as much as her father by managing and investing his money.

She went straight to her room when she arrived home. Her bedroom was just as she remembered leaving it. She rearranged it. She was no longer the person who had put up the posters and other pictures. She put away most of the pictures of people that she now no longer associated with.

She did not have many replacement pictures and no posters.

She decided to engage her mother and learn how her mother had gotten into managing what she was certain were millions of dollars.

Her mother responded very positively and went to great lengths to explain the process of becoming a certified money manager.

Mandy went into a listen but don't respond mode when her mother explained the six-month, eight hour a day curriculum required for certification.

She knew immediately that she was not up to that kind of concentration to get a certificate that would then allow her to work for other people.

She needed to focus on marrying a person with enough money that she might manage. Then maybe she would take such a course.

Then at a party she was introduced to Ralph Emanual Donaldson. He was a producer! He was handsome and somewhere between her age and her fathers.

She spent the evening getting to know him better and making sure that she ended up with a way to get back together with him.

She made sure to put some fire into their affair. She now had a goal in mind and planned to accomplish it.

She set about making sure they reconnected.

The day after the party her father approached her with a job a friend was offering her.

Mandy agreed to the job of being a business assistant, if her father would help her get into her own apartment.

She knew that pursuing Ralph from her parent's home would be an impossible task.

She gave her father a big hug when he agreed.

She learned that her mother was also happy to get into her own apartment.

The friend, Henry Rambler, was one of her father's college friends that were considered old Cincinnati money. His father had established the initial family wealth, and Henry had increased it with his home building and the reality business.

Mandy found him easy to work for but the work rather boring. However, the salary was generous, and it allowed her to be free from her parents support and watchful eye.

She was free to manage her own affairs.

It only took a couple of months for her to realize that Ralph was not a movie producer.

The people that surrounded Ralph came into focus. They were all in the drug business. The friendliest one, Bradley, was clearly a bodyguard. Severe acne had made his face more pock marked than the face of the moon. He was disfigured to the point of being hard to look at.

She had made it a point to greet him and chat with him. She learned he was from a small town in Mississippi and had been raised by his single mother.

Ralph was great in bed and was constantly varying his approach.

She picked up the bad habit of snorting cocaine but kept it at a social level and only did so when she was with Ralph.

It gave her the extra energy to keep up with him.

She figured that the relationship, based almost wholly on sex was doomed but she was not ready to leave.

She did not have an alternative.

Then one evening when they were enjoying a casual cup of after dinner tea, she noticed a sudden change.

Ralph seemed to stiffen as a stranger walked into the bar area.

She decided to excuse herself.

On her way to the lady's room, she saw Ralph nod at Bradley and watched his thumbs up reply.

Some instinctive response made her walk past the lady's room and out the side exit door.

She decided to get out of the area. She walked briskly to the corner and turned left toward the interstate. She thought about hitching a ride to get out of the area.

She stopped at the corner and saw a car coming out of the parking lot. She took her high heels off and began to run.

An old man walked slowly along the walk ahead of her. The squeal of tires filled the air from behind her.

She hit the old guy as she passed him. She heard him call after her but did not get what he was saying.

She had her eyes set on the far side of the bridge where she hoped there would be a way down to the highway.

The car pulled up ahead and screeched to a nosedive like stop and the front door opened. Bradley stepped out and used his massive shoulders to knock her into the wall.

The impact against the wall stunned her. She could barely see but she heard him say he was sorry and then felt him pick her up.

Bradley kept repeating that he was sorry.

The last thing she remembered was the surge upward and then falling, falling, falling.

Mandy had pursued the path she thought was an easy, fast, way to fame and fortune. Her poor choices in the end cost her, her life. Her parents raised a spoiled child that never learned the value of standing on her own and on the principle of working hard that had guided them.

Thank You for reading this far.

Purchase the Girl on the Grill at

https://Remwriter95.net/

About the Author

Ronald E. Mueller
remwriter95@gmail.com

Ron grew up in what is now Flint River State Park in Southeast Iowa. The 170-year-old house Ron lived in is built into a hillside. It faces a 125-foot-high cliff towering over the little Flint River. The house and the land talked to him about; the passing of time, the struggle to conquer the land, the struggles people faced and the wonder of nature.

He climbed the cliffs, crawled into the caves, dove from the swimming rock, collected clams from the bottom of the pond, gigged and skinned frogs for their legs. He trapped muskrats for fur, hunted raccoon in the dead of night, and with only a stick hunted rabbits in the dead of winter.

His young life was outdoors, and nature tested him.

He walked to a one room stone schoolhouse uphill both ways. A stern but warm-hearted teacher, Mrs. Henry was instrumental in shaping his character as she shepherded him from the fourth to the eighth grade.

It was a great way to grow up.

Ron graduated from Burlington, High School, went to Vietnam in the Navy. He graduated from The University of South Florida with a master's degree in engineering, worked for thirty eight years for Procter and Gamble, traveled around the world thirty times.

He has remained happily married for more than fifty years. His daughter and his two sons are all successful and his three grandchildren have all graduated.

His wife has humored and supported him as he became a full time became a professional story teller.

His experiences inter-twined with snippets of fantasy lend themselves to the adventures he leads the reader through.

Books by Ron Mueller

Fiction Series
The Alex Evercrest Series
> The River Front
> The Girl on The Grill
> Missing
> Maggot
> Racist
> Votive Candles
> Windy City
> Country Road
> Pool of Blood
> Sins of the Daughter
> Body Parts
> The Skull Collector
> The Vanishing
> The Shadow Fighter
> Moonshine
> Grief's Trajectory
> The Magic Touch
> Northern Lights
> Alex Evercrest Heroine
> Alex Evercrest Collection Two
> New Direction
> A Family Affair
> Disruption
> The St. Lebuinnus Church Murder

A Brian O'Neil Novel
> Hawaiian Phoenix
> Moon Curser
> Death Broker

The Problem Solver Series
> Solutions
> Drug Lords
> Border Crosser
> The Problem Solver Collection

The Taelo Series
Taelo: The Early Years
Taelo: The Golden Feather
Taelo: Journey of Discovery
Taelo: Dangerous Passage
Taelo: Condor Clan Slingers
Taelo: Circumvention
Taelo: The Journey of Sages
Taelo: Collection
Taelo: Future Leaders Journey

A Taelo Story:
White Swan and Quiet Pheasant
The Child's Name
Floating Cloud
Quiet Rabbit
Busy Bee
Little Otter & Talking Wren
Broken Spear
Burley Bear & Meadow Flower
Taelo Story Collection

Science Fiction

The Savitar Series:
Journey's End
Savitar
Confluence
Savitar Series Collection

Bram Nielson Series
The Fold
The Message
Fold Wormhole
Negative Fold
Ripples in Time
Bram Nielson Collection

Single Science Fiction Books:
Current Past and Future
The Event
The Door
Viajante 7

Published by: Around the World Publishing LLC

https://www.Remwriter95.net/

www.ingramcontent.com/pod-product-compliance
Lightning Source LLC
Chambersburg PA
CBHW070529100726
47907CB00004B/1046